Elliot didn't want to believe it,

but he seemed to have no choice. "Your job seems to call you at odd hours. I don't suppose I could... hire you myself."

"I don't think you could afford me," George said, unaware that her teasing was not being returned in kind.

Elliot stopped dead in his tracks, grasped her arms and pulled her around to face him. "Just how much do you charge?"

She finally understood. Oddly, his suspicions didn't make her angry, they made her want to laugh. "Well," she said softly, "I used to charge by the hour. But now, since my...reputation has spread, I can get more money under contract."

Elliot dropped his hands to his sides, more disgusted with himself than with her. How else could George own a Porsche, a house and God knew what else? George herself was now furious. He really thought she was a hooker!

Dear Reader,

When two people fall in love, the world is suddenly new and exciting, and it's that same excitement we bring to you in Silhouette Intimate Moments. These are stories with scope, with grandeur. These characters lead the lives we all dream of, and everything they do reflects the wonder of being in love.

Longer and more sensuous than most romances, Silhouette Intimate Moments novels take you away from everyday life and let you share the magic of love. Adventure, glamour, drama, even suspense— these are the passwords that let you into a world where love has a power beyond the ordinary, where the best authors in the field today create stories of love and commitment that will stay with you always.

In coming months look for novels by your favorite authors: Maura Seger, Parris Afton Bonds, Elizabeth Lowell and Erin St. Claire, to name just a few. And whenever you buy books, look for all the Silhouette Intimate Moments, love stories *for* today's women *by* today's women.

Leslie J. Wainger
Senior Editor
Silhouette Books

Aftershocks
Catherine Coulter

Silhouette Intimate Moments

Published by Silhouette Books New York

America's Publisher of Contemporary Romance

SILHOUETTE BOOKS
300 E. 42nd St., New York, N.Y. 10017

ISBN: 0-373-07121-3

First Silhouette Books printing December 1985
Second printing January 1986

CATHERINE COULTER

has long been familiar to readers of Regency romances, as well as to fans of longer historical novels. With *Aftershocks*, she makes her entry into the contemporary romance genre. Catherine and her husband, Anton, a doctor, live in the San Francisco area, where she writes most of the time. When she takes time off she likes to spend it sailing, playing the piano and, of course, reading.

To Neff,
a.k.a. Laura Matthews,
Elizabeth Neff Walker and Elizabeth Walker,
a dear friend and a talented writer

Chapter 1

It's a base hit, George! Run!"

George threw down her bat and dashed toward first base. She kicked it with her sneakered toe and rounded toward second. She saw the center fielder scoop up the softball and sling it clumsily toward the second baseman. Doctors, she thought, panting slightly as she headed for third, do not even make for decent competition. She held up on third, and waved the victory sign toward her teammates on the sidelines.

"I've never seen a girl hit a softball like that," Dr. Elliot Mallory observed lazily to Dr. David Thornton.

"Is she one of the new residents?" David asked, gulping down another swallow of his cold beer.

"Not that I know of," Elliot said. He stretched his long legs and leaned back against a tree trunk. "Lord, it's hot today."

"It is July, you know, Elliot, and we are in the East Bay. Your blood's thinned out from living in San Francisco."

Elliot looked up at the crack of a bat against the ball and watched the girl run gracefully from third to home. He heard moans from the opposition. "I'd like to have seen her slide," he remarked.

David cocked an amused eyebrow at him. "She does have very long, very bare legs," he said, shading his eyes with his hand to get a better look at the girl, who was now laughing and joking with her teammates on the sideline. "You want to dab iodine on any scratches she'd get?"

Elliot laughed. "I can't see her well enough from here. She's probably someone's teenage daughter." He looked up as a shadow fell over his shoulder.

"What a couple of lazy slugs," Dr. Margaret Smith said, grinning down at the two men.

"Whoever heard of mixing gynecology residents with radiology residents at the annual picnic?" Elliot said. "I don't see you out there competing, Maggie. You or your chairman here."

"I haven't forgotten the sprained ankle I got from one of you macho men in our football game last year. Friendly touch game, ha!"

David shaded his eyes. "Looks like our star softball player with the long legs is headed for the volleyball court."

"She is very athletic," Margaret said, watching the girl stride gracefully alongside Dr. Randy Hansen, a new first-year radiology resident.

"Hi, guys," Doris Thornton said gaily. She kicked her husband lightly in the ribs. "Come on, jock, it's time to show your stuff. They're choosing sides for volleyball and I want the chance to cream both of you.

"Go get 'em, Doris," Maggie laughed, "I'll be your cheering section."

Elliot fished his sunglasses out of his shirt pocket and slid them on. "I don't suppose you'll take maybe for an answer, Doris?" he asked, grinning up into her pixie face.

"No chance, you bum! Come on, both of you, or I'll burn your hamburgers!"

"Just so long as you don't burn our buns," David said, only to receive another toe on his ribs. He groaned, but struggled to his feet. "I'm too old for this."

Elliot joined him, and together they headed toward the court. Obligingly, Elliot and David took the opposite side of the court. Elliot, his six-foot-three-inch height a definite asset, started at the net, David, five-foot-eight in his shoes, beside him.

Elliot looked over the opposition, including Doris, who was making a face at them through the net, and said aloud to David, "No humiliation for us today, my man. Just a bunch of women."

"Don't let Doris hear you say that. She might be small, but she's mean." David laughed and practiced setting the volleyball to Elliot.

George's eyes narrowed. She was pulling the net taut and heard the comment. Conceited jerk! "Hey, Randy," she said to the slender young man who was standing at the net. "Let me trade places with you, all right?"

Randy Hansen shrugged. "Sure, George." His gray eyes narrowed against the bright sun. "I don't like it, though. You won't come up to serve until almost last."

There were nine players on each team, and seven of the players on George's team were women.

"Let the weaker sex begin!" David called out. "With my wife serving it will be a piece of cake."

Doris stuck out her tongue at her husband and caught the volleyball from George. "Lay it on 'em, Doris," George said.

Doris served the ball high and soft, right to her husband. He set it smoothly, and in the next instant, George saw the man with the big mouth leap up gracefully and slam the ball down behind her. There were boos and shouts from both teams, and Maggie shouted encouragement from the sideline.

George cocked her head to one side and examined the man anew. She liked what she saw. He was exceptionally tall and well built, with wide shoulders, a lean waist and firm, thick thighs. His thick black hair curled loosely about his head. He moved with the natural grace of an athlete. But he had to be a doctor, she supposed, frowning slightly. She and Randy had arrived late, and she hadn't met him. She wished she could see his eyes, but his sunglasses were darkly tinted.

The other team served, and a woman in the middle row struck at the ball wildly, sending it flying out of bounds. The next serve was short, barely clearing the net. George, a smile on her lips, timed her jump well and smashed the ball right into the man's face.

The sunglasses cracked and slid from his nose, and she stared into beautiful leaf-green eyes, staring back at her in mute surprise. He was undoubtedly a splendid male specimen. George, who knew little enough about flirting, reacted in the only way she knew.

She challenged him.

"It might help if you keep awake!" she shouted, laughing.

To her delight, the man grinned widely, showing even white teeth.

"George," Randy wailed from behind her, "don't insult my boss!"

"Well," George said, "I hope he's a better doctor than a volleyball player." She sent Randy's boss a dazzling smile.

Elliot wasn't insulted, he was amused and intrigued. He studied the girl across the net as the game continued haphazardly around him. She wasn't a teenager, but she was young, early twenties, he guessed, and incredibly lovely. She was tall, with slim, straight tanned legs that seemed to go on forever. Her hair, a deep honey color, was pulled back from her flawless face into a bedraggled ponytail. She wore no makeup and looked as clean and fresh as sunshine. He wondered, cynically, if her hair was dyed.

As both teams rotated to change servers, he glanced over her body. She wore a T-shirt with Beau Jangles across the chest and cutoff jeans. He watched her set the ball smoothly and easily, and watched her breasts rise as she jumped. He wanted to meet her.

"Hey, Elliot," David called to him. "Wake up! The game's nearly over."

Elliot waved his hand toward David, then turned to watch her move to the service line. His team was leading by an easy thirteen to five score. She handled the ball easily, and that should have warned him. In the next moment, the ball whizzed straight at him, low and hard. A man's serve. She caught him unawares, and the ball bounced off his belly onto the ground. He heard her laugh and her teammates cheer wildly.

"Bet you can't do that again!" David shouted out. Her next serve nearly flattened him with its speed and force.

Elliot was so busy laughing that he again missed the ball that was served straight at him. He settled down and managed her next serve, but Hoover, a third-year resident, bobbled it.

He heard her shout, "Practice makes perfect!" and took the serve again. When his team finally managed to return the ball, Doris, in a stroke of blind luck, struck it with the palm of her hand and got it back over.

George sent every couple of serves to him, until finally he didn't set the ball but sent it over himself, straight at her. She gave a shout of laughter and set it clean and high. His team lost another point. When the score stood at 13-13, Elliot's competitive spirit could stand no more. He took the serve again and set it over the net into Randy's chest. He saw the girl leap forward for a save, but she missed it. She's good, he thought with satisfaction, very good.

He took the volleyball from David and strolled to the serving line, smiling at the shouts of "Kill, kill" from his teammates.

He grinned wickedly, knowing she was ready for him. Usually when playing with women, he underhanded his serve. Now, he tossed it in the air, and smashed it hard and low, right at her. She set it easily, but her team lost the point.

"Game point for the bad guys!" Maggie called out from the sideline.

Elliot gave the girl a little salute and sent her another ball harder than the last one. Like him, she took no chance, and returned the ball herself from the back row. His teammate hit it into the net.

Groans issued from Elliot's team, and the women chortled gleefully, for George was back at the net. Doris served and Hoover, flustered, barely managed to return it, right into George's waiting hand. She smashed it to the ground. Her team made the last point on a fluke.

There was crowing and good-natured grumbling. Elliot walked slowly to Randy, who had just whirled the girl around in his arms.

"How 'bout an introduction to the jock, Dr. Hansen?" he drawled.

George turned to face him and felt her cheeks grow warm. It was an odd feeling, one she had never experienced before, and she stared at him vaguely, wondering how anyone could make another feel so fluttery.

"Georgina Hathaway," Randy said, clearing his throat, "this is Dr. Elliot Mallory, Chairman of Radiology, and my *boss*."

"You're not bad, for a doctor," she said, and stretched out her hand for him to shake.

"And you're not so bad yourself, for a girl," he said, and he clasped her slender hand firmly. There was no wedding band on his finger. She prayed he wasn't married.

"A poor loser, doctor. I am disappointed."

"And I am without my sunglasses. I trust you will buy me another pair?"

"Of course she will, won't you, George?" Randy said, his eyes narrowing on her upturned face.

George merely laughed and turned back to Dr. Mallory. "I'll do better than that, sir. I have two tickets to the A's baseball game next Tuesday. I'll take you."

Elliot blinked. The girl had just asked him out! "What if I said I would prefer new sunglasses, Miss Hathaway?"

Randy, who had never before seen George even interested in a man, stood helplessly by, gaping at her.

"Well," George said thoughtfully, her eyes never leaving Elliot's face, "I suppose I would have to offer you the sunglasses as a bribe."

Elliot couldn't help himself. He laughed, throwing his head back.

"Of course," George added, enjoying the sound of his deep rumbling laughter, "if you hadn't been sleeping, you wouldn't have lost them in the first place."

Elliot threw up his hands, his palms spread in defeat. "Next Tuesday, Miss Hathaway. Dr. Hansen, take care that no one strangles her until then." He smiled again, and took his parting shot before walking away. "If I hadn't lost my glasses, Miss Hathaway, you wouldn't have a bribe."

He laughed when she blinked at him, finally at a loss for a comeback. He heard Randy Hansen say to her, "George, have you lost your mind? Jesus, I've never seen you act like that. He's a very important man, and here you are flirting with him!"

There was a moment of silence, then an angry, "I don't flirt, Randy! Come on, let's eat. Then I've got to get home and see to my scraped knee. What Ben will say when he sees it, I can only imagine! If my lips get chapped, he curses in three languages!"

Who the hell is Ben, Elliot Mallory wondered. Her boyfriend, her lover? Not her husband; she wore no wedding band either. To his disappointment, she kept her distance the rest of the afternoon.

The following Tuesday morning, Elliot Mallory entered the ultrasound room where Randy Hansen was doing his first rotation. He waited silently until Randy finished reading out for Dr. Gordon.

"Dr. Mallory!"

"Good morning, Randy," Elliot said pleasantly. "I trust you're finding your residency less trying than your internship."

"I'm enjoying it, sir. Especially the eight hours of sleep every night."

Elliot questioned him politely for a while, then asked, as if as an afterthought, "The A's game is this evening, Dr. Hansen. I haven't heard from Miss Hathaway. Perhaps you can give me her phone number and I'll give her a call."

Randy felt his face flush in embarrassment. "Her number is unlisted, sir. I don't have it. I'm sorry."

"No matter," Elliot said easily. "She was likely serious that she would take me, and not the other way around. I shouldn't have worried about it. Good day, Dr. Hansen."

Randy watched Dr. Mallory walk out of the reading room, and sank down in the nearest chair.

"What was that all about, Randy?" his friend, Dr. Morgan, asked.

"Nothing, Tom." Jesus, Randy thought, what the hell was George doing, anyway? He had raked her over the coals on their drive back to San Francisco after the picnic. "How could you come on like that to a man like Dr. Mallory!" he had railed at her, nearly sideswiping a Volkswagen in his righteous ire. "He's over thirty-five, for God's sake, and you can bet he isn't used to some snitty girl asking him out! He's my chief, George! He's probably wondering how the hell to get out of it.''

She had looked at him thoughtfully. "Perhaps you're right," she had said in a low voice, surprising him so much with her instant capitulation that he had left her alone.

And now she hadn't called Dr. Mallory and likely the man would blame him for it!

"Damn," he muttered, and flung an ultrasound film up on the alternator.

Elliot returned to his office. His secretary, Lisa Dickerson, greeted him with her motherly smile.

"You were only gone for fifteen minutes, and there are three messages." She handed them to him and watched him sort through them. He paused over one and raised his head.

"When did Miss Hathaway call, Lisa?"

"About ten minutes ago."

"What exactly did she say?"

Lisa frowned, shaking her head. "It was odd, really. She didn't ask for you, just asked if she could leave a message for you. All she said was that she was in New York and apologized for not letting you know sooner."

"Nothing else?"

"No. Is anything wrong, doctor?"

Elliot looked at the crumpled message in his fist. "No, Lisa. Call back Dr. Bailey, will you? And get Dr. Dunsmuir down here. I want to talk to him about his paper on mitral valve prolapse. He's got to clean it up before he can submit it for publication.''

That afternoon, a small package was delivered to Elliot's office. Inside it was a very expensive pair of sun cloud sunglasses. What is she doing in New York, he wondered, as he tried the sunglasses on. They fit perfectly.

For the rest of the week, Elliot found himself on the verge of asking Randy Hansen for Georgina Hathaway's address. But he didn't.

Chapter 2

George pulled on her dark green Speedo swimsuit and her white swim cap. Her hands were shaking a bit. She stuck out her tongue at herself in the mirror in the women's dressing room, turned and walked into the pool area.

It was nearly one o'clock and there were six swimmers in the heated pool, lane swimming. She adjusted her goggles and slipped into the water, taking the middle lane. She swam one lap, then paused to look around her. The doctors and staff who swam here were serious about it, grinding out their laps with fierce concentration. She looked toward the men's dressing room, then forced herself to swim another lap.

"Hi, Dr. Mallory," she heard Tim say, the young giant who worked as lifeguard and pool cleaner.

She was treading water in the deep end of the pool when she saw him. There could be no more beautiful man, she thought, her eyes sweeping over his body.

She paused at his flat belly and swallowed, picturing the line of black hair that disappeared beneath his brief dark blue swim trunks. His legs were powerful, his thighs thick with muscle. He paused a moment at the edge of the pool and stretched. George swallowed a mouthful of water. He adjusted his goggles, dived cleanly into the water and set out on his laps.

George kicked off the deep-end wall and swam toward him in the lane next to his. He passed her with powerful strokes and had almost caught up with her by the time she reached the shallow end of the pool. She watched him turn smoothly and kick off into another lap. Now that he was here, and she was here, she didn't know what to do. She had joined the Milton Union the month before under Randy's name and had managed to swim a couple of mornings a week. She knew Elliot came every day at one o'clock, swam for precisely thirty minutes, spent another fifteen in the sauna and went back to the hospital across the street.

Well, she decided finally, surprise was her best approach. She set out on another lap, purposefully swimming in his lane. They collided in the middle of the pool in a thrash of arms and legs.

George sputtered and yelled, "Lane hog!"

Elliot blinked at the woman, saw that she was clearly in his lane and said acidly, "If you can't swim a straight line, perhaps you better move to the side lane."

"Ha!" she said, eyeing him joyfully. "You shouldn't be swimming here at all. Perhaps you better wait until three o'clock and join the beginners!"

Elliot pulled off his goggles, stunned at the insult. He gritted his teeth. "Excuse me, " he said finally, and kicked off without putting on his goggles again.

"Even now you're veering into my lane," she yelled after him.

Elliot heard her. Without pause, he whipped around in the water and swam in quick angry strokes back to the obnoxious woman.

"Now look here," he began. His tongue stuck in his throat when the woman pulled off her goggles, and he found himself staring at Georgina Hathaway.

"You look quite ridiculous," George said on a laugh. "Close your mouth." Her arms shot out to his shoulders and she shoved him underwater.

George knew she shouldn't have done it in the middle of the deep end, but she couldn't help herself. She felt his hands on her waist, and in the next instant she was flailing underwater. He brought her up, his hands still about her waist.

"Hi," George said cheerfully, wiping her eyes. "What are you doing here?"

Elliot eyed her suspiciously. "I suspect," he said, "that you knew I was here. Couldn't you just have said hello instead of attacking me?"

"You were very polite. It took that last insult to bring you back." She cocked her head to one side, very aware that he was still holding her, treading water for the both of them. "What were you going to say?"

"I haven't the faintest notion. Doubtless I would have thought of something appropriate to say to an obnoxious female."

"Well, even though you really weren't pigging my lane, you were swimming dreadfully slow. A Mack truck in neutral could have passed you. I could probably beat you with one leg."

"If I engage in a race with you, Miss Hathaway, will you knock off my goggles?"

"No, it won't be necessary. Now you know, from painful experience, that I'm not to be trifled with."

He grinned at her. "Come along then. How many laps would you like to try?"

She dog-paddled next to him toward the shallow end. She was not a good swimmer; it was one of the few sports she hadn't grown up with. "How about ten laps?" She had never even done ten laps. By six, her arms were like dead sticks of wood.

"Ten it is," said Elliot. "Would you like to dive to begin?"

"Certainly. This is a professional competition, at least my half is."

He watched her pull herself from the pool in a quick graceful motion. He found himself staring at her when she stood. A racing swimsuit on a woman was usually the most sexless garment imaginable. It fit like a second skin, flattening a woman's breasts and molding quite clearly every extra pound she carried. On George, the second skin revealed perfection. He felt his body respond, and tensed. He dragged his eyes away from her nipples, puckered against the suit, only to let them fall to her narrow waist and flat stomach. He quickly looked away, so as to be able to get out of the pool without embarrassing himself.

He joined her at the edge of the pool, seeing her long, beautiful legs bent, ready to dive.

"You look very sexy in that swimsuit," she said in a throaty voice, her eyes sweeping over him. At his sharp intake of breath, she shouted, "Go!"

Elliot watched her dive, and smiled at her clean, perfect form. He shook his head and dived in after her. He caught her on the second lap. Instead of passing, he slowed and kept pace with her. Her strokes were becoming more and more labored.

"I've never raced a snail before," he said.

"Snake," she said breathlessly. "Would you just go along and get it over with?"

"Not on your life. If I finish the ten laps, you'll be able to stop. I want to see if you can even make eight."

He thought she said "Jerk," but he couldn't be certain. She did make seven, but when she turned to begin the eighth, he pulled at her arm.

"I just wanted to humiliate you, not kill you," he said.

"I'm humiliated, and half-dead." She lowered her head, concentrating on breathing normally again. They were standing in the shallow end, and she was looking, mesmerized, at the black hair on his chest.

"When did you start swimming?"

"Last month."

"Why?"

"I always start something new in August."

"Why didn't you call me?"

She didn't pretend to misunderstand. "I did."

"No, you called my secretary."

"I was in New York."

"This is the first time I've seen you here."

"I know. Usually I swim in the morning. I was...surprised to see you here."

A black brow arched upward. "Were you now? I wonder."

"Your conceit, as well as a lot more, is showing."

"Only to my waist," he murmured, grinning at her wickedly. To his further amusement, she blushed. "Would you like to sit out for a while before we finish your humiliation?"

She cupped a handful of water, tossed it into his face and pulled herself out of the pool.

"Thank you for the sunglasses," he said, once he had joined her.

"You like them? I thought they looked classy."

"Quite classy and quite expensive, much more so than the ones you wrecked."

She smiled. "Well, Randy told me how *important* you are. Can't have you looking like a punk rocker."

Elliot looked out over the pool for a moment. "I would say they'd be quite an extravagant purchase on a student's budget, Miss Hathaway."

"I'm not a student, and please call me George. Everyone does."

"How did you ever get tangled up with a name like that? The San Francisco influence?"

"Oh no. I have three older brothers, and they think of me as their little brother."

"So that's why you're a jock."

"They just refined my jockdom. I was born with it."

"Except for swimming."

"Alas, you're right. I probably won't be able to beat you until Christmas."

"We'll see about that...George. Why aren't you in school?"

She smiled at him, but didn't immediately answer him. She pulled off her swim cap. Tendrils of wet hair fell about her face from the thick knot of honey-colored hair on top of her head. "I dropped out at the end of the first semester of my freshman year. I was bored, and studying the life cycle of frogs seemed a total waste."

Elliot looked at her hair for a moment; then his eyes fell to her face. She wore no makeup. He decided that with her delicate bones, she would be beautiful when she was eighty.

"You're thinking about all the years you spent in the academic grind," she teased him.

"Not exactly," he said. "What do you do with your time?"

George shrugged, a tiny smile playing about her lips. "Oh, a bit of this and that."

"I'm sorry we didn't make the A's game. I was looking forward to it."

She glanced at him through her thick lashes. "Are you putting me on?"

He raised a muscled arm and made the sign of an X over his chest. "Nope. I was in a foul mood for the rest of the day." He paused a moment, a smile widening his mouth. "I think I scared the hell out of Dr. Hansen when he told me he didn't have your phone number."

"Yes," she said, "you did. He bitched at me for a week."

"Why is you number unlisted?"

"I...enjoy my privacy."

"I see." But he didn't. "What were you doing in New York?"

Again he saw the teasing smile about her mouth.

"Ah, more of this and that?"

"That's it exactly," she said. "I am sorry about our aborted outing. I wanted to take you, but Randy, well, he burned my ears all the way back to San Francisco after the picnic."

Elliot arched a thick black brow in question.

She made a small gesture with her hand. "You're a very important man, Dr. Mallory," she said, mimicking Randy. "And you really didn't want to go, but were too polite to tell me to buzz off."

"I wouldn't count on that, George."

"Count on what?"

"On my being polite. Do you think you can get hold of another couple of tickets?"

She turned a happy smile on him and he blinked. "Isn't there anything ugly about you?" he asked. "A disfiguring mole somewhere or something?"

George gave a gurgling laugh. "I could ask you the same question, you know. It's my stock in trade, but for you it's a bonus."

"Did your brothers teach you to say things like that to strange men?"

She looked away from him, and he could see her slender shoulders stiffen. "Randy said that you wouldn't understand. I'm sorry."

"Dr. Hansen is a fool. Now, how about an A's game and a disfiguring mole?"

"How about Thursday and I don't have one."

"Thursday it is and I'm not sure I believe you. No woman should look like you do. It's unhealthy."

"Well," George said, untangling herself and standing over him, presenting him with the length of her endless legs, "I will pick you up on Thursday at seven. And I'll paint on a mole if you like."

"I'd prefer finding it for myself, thank you."

Her eyes, the oddest shade of blue, almost violet, widened. He wondered if he embarrassed her, but that hardly seemed likely. She seemed so sure of herself, so very sophisticated. And now she was looking at him uncertainly. Was she already regretting chasing him down?

"Do you know where I live?"

"Yes. You're in the book. I've got to go now. Goodbye."

"See you Thursday," he called after her. He watched her walk over to where Tim was standing, that young man looking anything but bored as he watched her approach. Elliot slipped back into the pool to continue his laps.

During the next two days, he found himself wondering if she would show up on Thursday. He had responded to her unabashed flirting in kind. At least he thought she'd been flirting with him. She certainly said anything she wanted to. She was very young, he thought. If and when he did see her again, he would take great pains not to scare her off. And what, he kept wondering, did she mean about this and that?

Elliot heard the doorbell ring at precisely seven o'clock. Somehow, he had expected her to be punctual. He galloped down the stairs and opened the door.

"Hi," George said.

"Hello," Elliot said. "You look very nice." Actually he would like to have told her that she looked good enough to eat, but wisely swallowed the words. She was wearing a light-blue silk blouse and tan slacks, and her hair was drawn away from her face with combs. He realized he was staring at her and said quickly, "Would you like to come in for a drink?"

"No," George replied. "It's a forty-minute drive to the stadium. I don't want to be late."

He pulled the door closed and followed her down the steps. He came to a surprised halt at the sight of a black Porsche parked in the driveway. It was a classic 911, about ten years old, in perfect condition. He smiled as she opened the door on the passenger's side for him. "Nice car," he said, eyeing the black-leather interior.

George didn't reply until she slipped into the driver's seat. "Yes," she said proudly. "Her name is Esmerelda."

"Is the hunchback of Notre Dame in the back seat?"

"I told him I only had two tickets. He has to wait for another night." She revved the engine and expertly shoved the gear stick into reverse.

"How long have you had her?"

"I bought her in February."

How the hell, he wondered, could a girl her age, who did this and that, afford a car that must have cost at least twenty thousand dollars? He fastened his seat belt and watched her take the hills in Pacific Heights. She stopped behind a car on a steep incline, and he found himself stiffening. Driving a stick shift in San Francisco required guts and skill. She certainly had the latter, he thought, expelling his breath as she expertly shifted the Porsche into first and smoothly eased forward.

"I won't wreck you," George said dryly. "Women are much maligned about their driving."

"I was too busy wondering where I had put my will to malign you."

She laughed and shot him an impish look. "Just wait until we get to a flat stretch. I'll have Esmerelda do her stuff."

She negotiated the freeway traffic like a pro, and they were soon on the Bay Bridge. "What kind of car do you drive?" she asked. She quickly raised a slender hand. "No, let me guess. A Continental? A Cadillac Seville?"

"Wrong. A silver Jaguar, and yes, my mechanic is a very good friend."

"A stick shift?"

"Yes, but I must admit to stalling *him* on hills occasionally."

"I'm sure you do very well...for a man."

"I didn't have the benefit of having three sisters."

She giggled. "You are funny. I thought you would be. Are you a native Californian?"

"There are so few, I wish I could claim to be one, but I'm not. I was born and grew up in Connecticut."

"I have a friend in Stamford. Near there?"

"In the east, everything is close to everything else. New Milford, and in answer to your next question, I went to Yale."

"Actually, I was hoping you would say Harvard. Harvard is more snooty, isn't it?"

"Any Harvard alumnus would agree, I'm sure. How 'bout you, George?"

"My folks live in Flint, Michigan. My aborted semester of college was at the University of Michigan."

"What did you do after that? You were all of eighteen, right?"

"Yes. I lived in New York, then came out here. I've lived in San Francisco for about two years now."

"If I recall right, Dr. Hansen went to Columbia. You met him in New York?"

"Yes," she said shortly. "We're almost there, Dr. Mallory. I do hope you like baseball."

"You may be certain I like hot dogs and peanuts."

"I know the vendor. You'll put on a couple of pounds tonight."

"I'll swim it off with you tomorrow."

She shot him a questioning look, but was soon concentrating on entering the parking lot. Instead of parking in the public area, she drove to the reserved section very close to the entrance. All the places were taken except for one. She pulled smoothly in and turned off the motor.

As if in answer to his unasked question, she smiled and said only, "Since I'm bringing such an important man, you get only the best."

She led him briskly to the ticket counter.

"Hi, George."

"Hi, Dave. Here's the tickets."

"What happened to the other fellow, George?"

"Dr. Hansen is only a resident. This fellow is far more important. He runs the whole show."

The older man grinned widely at her, showing a wide space between his front teeth. "Only the best, huh, George?"

Elliot wasn't at all surprised when she led him directly behind home plate to some of the best seats in the stadium.

"A pretty good turnout," George said with satisfaction, glancing around the stadium. "We'll kill the Yankees, maybe."

Nor was he particularly surprised when a boy, a tray of hot dogs strapped to his shoulders, hailed her like a long-lost friend. He listened with half an ear to their conversation, only paying full attention when he said, "Tod's in good shape, isn't he, George?"

"Perfect shape," George said firmly, taking two hot dogs from him. "And he's raring to go tonight."

Elliot was pulling out his wallet to pay for the hot dogs when the boy waved him down. "No, sir. George gets anything she wants."

George grinned at him. "You, Dr. Mallory, are the power at the hospital. I am the power at the stadium."

"So I see," Elliot said dryly. "Do you own part of the A's?"

She seemed to consider his question seriously. "Not yet. Perhaps in a couple of years. We'll see."

"George," he began, a definite edge to his voice.

"Shh, the national anthem."

When the A's pitcher took the mound, Elliot sat back in his chair, his arms crossed over his chest, and prepared to be bored. He was not a baseball fan. He was bored until the pitcher looked straight at them and waved.

"Go get 'em, Tod!" George yelled, and the pitcher gave her a victory sign.

"There's both a Tod and a Ben?" Elliot growled.

George turned to him, her head cocked to one side. Her lovely hair fell forward over her shoulder.

"How do you know about Ben?"

"I heard you mention him to Dr. Hansen."

"Oh. Yes, there's both a Tod and a Ben. Do you know that Tod's fastball has been clocked at over ninety-five miles an hour?"

Before he could answer, George was on her feet, cheering a strike.

Elliot took a vicious bite of his hot dog.

"All right," George said finally, taking pity on him, "I've been putting you on. If you were a baseball fan, which I gather you're most definitely not, you would know that the pitcher is Tod Hathaway. He's my brother.''

Elliot stared at her, then leaned back and laughed. His first thought was that that left only Ben. ''How are you at wrestling?'' he asked pleasantly.

''I'm better at judo,'' George said. ''If you're thinking about beating me up, you'd best think again.''

''Where the hell did you learn judo?''

''You forget, I have —''

''Yes, I know. You have three brothers. Now we've accounted for one of them. Are the others boxers or football players?''

''Alas no. But I still love them. Derek, the oldest, is a businessman, and Jason is a computer expert. Tod, however, is the star of the family.''

''What about you, George?''

''Me? I'm still a faint light on the horizon.''

''You have a lovely home,'' George said as she pulled into his driveway.

''Thank you. Would you like to see the inside?''

''I'd like to, but I have to get home to bed. I've got a hard day tomorrow.''

''Where do you live?''

She gave him a twinkling smile. ''About a mile from you, on Broadway. It's not a beautiful Victorian like yours, but it's mine.''

''You *own* your own home?''

''A condo. Three bedrooms, and quite sufficient for me.''

''George, how old are you?''

''Twenty-three. Why?''

"When I was twenty-three, I lived in a hole in the wall and ate beans for supper. And I owned an old Chevy Impala."

"Yes, but you were busy educating yourself for the future. I, on the other hand, am still quite ignorant. I hope you enjoyed the game, even though Tod lost."

"Yes, I did," he said, accepting her change of subject philosophically. "Will you come to the pool tomorrow?"

"I'll be free by then, hopefully. Thanks a lot for coming with me."

He looked at her outstretched hand, then clasped it in his. "My pleasure, George." He stood on the front porch until Esmerelda roared out of sight.

She wasn't at the pool the next day, and Elliot, coming out of the water after a full hour, his toes and fingers wrinkled as prunes, realized he still didn't have her damned phone number.

Chapter 3

"Toss your head, George! That's it, baby, chin up. I wanna see your long neck."

"I feel like a giraffe," George called out to Clyde, but obligingly did as he directed.

"I want men to want to smell the perfume on your neck. Turn your head a bit, as if you're inviting that special man closer."

George thought of Elliot and proceeded to invite him.

"Beautiful!" Click, click, click. The whir of the camera was the only sound on the set.

Ben Bernstein sat back and folded his hands over his comfortable stomach. George had more class and pizazz than *Charlie* any day, he thought, inordinately pleased with himself, and with her. Next week she would be presented by the PR people at Braden-Tyrol House as herself, Georgina, their top model and representative for all their cosmetics and perfumes. Bra-

den-Tyrol didn't even mind that George was allergic
to perfume; as for their makeup, George, a health nut
to his mind, hadn't balked all. Thank God and their
scientists for those natural ingredients with weird
names Ben couldn't begin to pronounce.

Ben watched her toss her head seductively again toward Clyde; the shimmery purple in the dress she wore
caught the violet lights in her eyes. Smart cookie, his
George. Unlike his other models, George had set her
own terms and, through him, had negotiated her very
lucrative three-year contract.

"Is that it, Clyde? Is it noon yet?"

"Hell no, George. Where you been? It's nearly one-
thirty now."

George felt like punching him out. She sent a re-
proachful look toward Ben. She had told both Clyde
and Ben that she had to leave the shoot by noon. No
wonder her beautiful giraffe neck felt like it would
break in two with fatigue. She tossed the vial of perfume toward Clyde and stalked off the set. "Thanks
for nothing," she called back over her shoulder.

Clyde's studio was on Lombard Street. Even driving fast enough to bring the San Francisco cops down
on her head, she wouldn't make it in time. She shook
a fist toward the two men, who were standing in jo-
vial conversation, the two of them looking for all the
world like a comedy team. Ben, short, plump and
balding, and Clyde, tall, skinny and redheaded. She
called them Coral and Hardly. Now she'd like to call
them vastly different names.

Well, she reasoned, after changing into jeans and a
pullover, Elliot would call her, and she would simply
explain that she had gotten tied up. *He can't call, you
idiot! He doesn't have your phone number!*

Here I go again, she sighed, resigned, chasing him again! She got his secretary, Lisa, on the phone.

"Is Dr. Mallory there?" George asked, trying to sound confident and professional.

"I'm sorry, but Dr. Mallory is in conference and can't be disturbed. May I tell him who called, or give him a message?"

George chewed on her lower lip. "Do you know when he will be free?" she hedged. Her voice sounded squeaky, like a teenager's, she thought, disgusted at herself.

Lisa Dickerson smiled into the phone. She recognized the woman's voice. It was the same woman who had put Dr. Mallory into an unaccustomed snit for several days the week before. "Miss Hathaway?" she inquired into the phone.

"Yes," George said.

"Ah. I believe that Dr. Mallory will be free and ready to leave the hospital around six o'clock this evening."

"Can one visit the hospital at six o'clock?"

"I think it can be arranged," Lisa said without a quiver. She then proceeded to give Miss Hathaway directions. When she hung up the phone, she vowed to stay late.

I can't keep running after him like this, George thought, dragging her feet slowly toward the hospital elevators. He'll think I'm a total jerk, that I'm infatuated with him. She managed to talk herself into a state of incoherent insecurity by the time she reached Dr. Elliot Mallory's office on the third floor. She gazed nervously at the sign on the oak door. Chairman of Radiology. She had turned and was on the

point of leaving when she heard a woman's voice behind her.

"Miss Hathaway?"

George spun around on her heels to face a tall, very
kind-looking woman about the age of her mother,
who was standing in the open doorway of Elliot's office.

"Yes," George managed, holding her position.

"You've come to the right place. Dr. Mallory is in
his office and should be through in just a couple of
minutes. Won't you come in?"

"Perhaps I shouldn't," George began, backing
away. "He's probably too busy."

"Nonsense," Lisa said cheerfully. She was having
a hard time not staring at the vision in those black
slacks and the dark-green silk blouse. Even her ears are
beautiful, she thought. No wonder Dr. Mallory had
tongue-lashed the entire staff. "Come along." Once
she had Miss Hathaway inside her office, she quickly
shut the outer door. "He's running a bit late," she
observed with a smile, "because he spent a longer time
at the pool today than usual."

"Oh," said George.

Dr. Mallory's door opened at that moment, and
Elliot emerged, wearing an expensive three-piece
charcoal-gray suit, and a pale-blue button-down shirt.
The man beside him wore a white coat and looked
nervous.

Elliot stopped in midgrowl, much to Dr. Dysan's
confusion and relief. "George," he said. "What the
hell are you doing here?"

George was on her feet in an instant. "I'm sorry. I
shouldn't have come and...bothered you. I'll leave
now. Goodbye."

"Just a moment. Sit down!"

George sat.

"Ralph, I believe we've finished for the day. Lisa, there is no need for you to...work any longer today. George, come in my office."

Just like a Nazi general, George thought, but she nonetheless walked past him into a beautifully furnished corner office, its ceiling-to-floor windows providing a magnificent view of the Bay and the Golden Gate Bridge. The room was paneled in dark wood, one wall covered with built-in bookcases, the other painted cream and covered with prints of ships. The desk, piled with papers, magazines and X-ray films, was a large, mahogany affair, probably a beautiful antique if enough of it could be seen. There was an inviting light brown leather sofa with two matching chairs flanking it. George walked to the windows.

She heard the door close.

"More of *this and that*?" came a sarcastic voice.

She turned and said blankly, "This and what?"

Elliot would have liked to fan his ire a bit longer, but he saw she was staring at him, her eyes traveling slowly down his body. He felt a shock of sheer lust and forgot his sense of ill-use.

He would have liked to toss her on the sofa and peel off her slacks. Instead, after she had completed her examination, he said, "I'm sorry I missed you today."

"I got...tied up. I wanted to speed over here, but the cops go crazy at the sight of a Porsche."

"Likely." He smiled. "They might have fancied themselves as Dirty Harrys. Are you hungry? Are you free for dinner?"

She gave him a delighted smile. "I'm relieved that you were the one to ask!"

"Would you like an omelette at Cliff House?"

"Fine with me." She hung back a moment, worried that perhaps he was just being polite to a pushy female. "Are you certain I'm not taking you away from something?"

"Yes, you are," he said, waving a dismissing hand toward the piles of papers on his desk, "and I appreciate it."

"I like your office," George said.

"Impressive enough for such an *important* fellow?"

She gave him a dimpled smile, and he gazed fondly again toward the sofa. "Are you ready?" he asked abruptly.

"Yes. I'll follow you in my car."

Elliot ushered her from his office and locked the door. "What tied you up?"

"My job."

He couldn't help the frown. "You seem to...be called at odd times."

"Not really," George said, aware of the sudden sarcasm in his voice but not understanding it. She cocked her head at him.

"I don't suppose," Elliot continued, not looking at her, "that I could...hire you myself."

"I don't think you could afford me," George said, still unaware that her teasing was not being returned in kind.

Elliot stopped dead in his tracks. He grasped her arms and pulled her around to face him. "Just how much do you charge?"

She finally understood. Oddly enough, his suspicion didn't make her angry, it made her want to laugh. She fluttered her eyelashes. "Well," she said in a soft voice, "I used to charge by the hour. But now, since my...reputation has spread, I can get more money under contract."

"Contract! Are you telling me that someone owns you exclusively?"

"Oh, never that," she assured him, watching his face flush darker with anger. "Say that a group hires me, not just one single person."

Elliot dropped his hands to his sides. He was more disgusted with himself than with her. How else could a girl as beautiful as George own a Porsche, a house and God knew what else?

"Is something wrong?" George inquired in what she thought sounded like a seductive voice.

"Yes," he snapped. "I just remembered that I have a meeting. I'll take you to your car."

He really thought she was a...hooker! She watched him punch the elevator button as if he wanted to kill it.

They rode to the lobby in silence.

"Just a moment, Dr. Mallory," George said. "Could you come here please?"

His frown didn't ease as he watched her pick up a magazine from the counter and quickly thumb through it. She set it down and picked up another.

"I suppose I've been putting you on," she said, turning to him, the magazine in her hand. "Here."

He took the magazine from her and looked down at the glossy color advertisement. George, dressed in a white jumpsuit, her hair piled high atop her head, smiled at him from the page. Behind her was a racetrack. In her hand she held a vial of perfume. "Jesus," he muttered. Slowly, feeling like an absolute fool, Elliot said, "You're a model."

"Yes, for five years now."

"Why the hell did you let me think that you were..."

"A hooker?" she supplied when he stalled. "Actually, once I realized what you thought, I decided to tease you a bit."

"What I thought isn't funny, George."

"No, not at all. Perhaps the next time you meet someone who just happens to be young and owns a Porsche, you won't jump to conclusions so quickly."

"I never would have thought anything of the sort if you hadn't made all sorts of glib, obscure comments. Oh, hell," he added, running his hand through his hair. "I'm sorry. Talk about being out in left field. Will you forgive my stupidity?"

"Yes, this time."

Elliot smiled at her ruefully. "Lord, let's get out of here. I see Dr. Stone coming. The man's a dead bore."

It took them fifteen minutes to get out of the hospital parking garage. George followed his silver Jaguar for a few minutes, then cut over to Clement Street. He was waiting for her outside Cliff House, and he wasn't smiling. So much for his apology, she thought. She'd given him too much time to chew over her part in making him draw the wrong conclusion. But living with three brothers had accustomed her to any male aberration involving their own sense of ill-use, and she didn't pay him much heed.

They were no sooner at their table looking out over the water than Elliot said stiffly, "I don't like games. Why didn't you simply tell me you're a model?"

She sipped thoughtfully on her Perrier. "You're right," she agreed readily. "I shouldn't have done it. Will you forgive me?"

She saw that he was torn. He felt like treating her to a livid tirade, but she had spiked his guns.

He hung on stoutly. "Then why did you do it? It was infantile."

"I didn't want you to think that I'm just a pretty face." She added candidly as she watched him chew over this bit of information, "You see, most men believe that if a woman looks good, especially if she's got blond hair, she's a dummy. When they find out she's a model, they're sure of it. I'm not a dummy."

A waiter appeared and George ordered her favorite number eight omelette, bacon and avocado. Elliot ordered a hangtown.

"Oh, no," George groaned suddenly. "And I did so much like coming here!"

Elliot looked up, perplexed, to see a stout woman with dubious red hair approaching their table. She was clutching a piece of paper and a pen. "Miss Hathaway? Miss Georgina Hathaway?"

"Yes," George said and took the paper and pen.

"Please write it to Agnes."

George nodded and scribbled on the paper.

"Oh, thank you, Miss Hathaway! Wait until I tell my sister! Such a thrill to see you in person!"

"Does that happen often?" Elliot asked after the woman had left.

"No," George said in a clipped voice.

Elliot reached his hand over the table and lightly touched his fingers to hers. "Forgive me, George."

George was staring at his long, blunt fingers and the sprinkling of black hair on the back of his hand. When he touched her, she blinked. She raised her head and gazed at his mouth, every delightful sensation she felt mirrored in her eyes.

"George," he began, "if you don't stop that, I'm going to throw you over my shoulder and haul you out of here! In fact," he continued in a husky voice that made shivers dance up and down her back, "...oh, damn!"

He withdrew his hand as the waiter set their omelettes down. George stared blankly at her plate. She felt shaken, breathless and tongue-tied. She decided she enjoyed it.

She watched him wolf down the omelette, knowing well what he was thinking. That shook her, too.

Even his wretched voice is sexy, she thought. It appeared she was going to get exactly what she wanted. But it was too soon. She had to know him better before she decided.

Elliot was taken aback when she began talking blandly about the seals on the rocks below. She had withdrawn, and he couldn't for the life of him understand why. He had never before been chased so blatantly, and with such beguiling sophistication. He wondered about a model's life; surely she had her pick of men. She was probably just out for a fling, and he fully intended not to disappoint himself or her.

"Yes, the seals are fascinating, aren't they?"

"Look at the spotted one! How old are you, Elliot?"

He blinked. "I'll be thirty-eight in January."

"Randy says you're very young to be a department chairman."

"True, but I'm also very bright." Elliot sat back in his chair to enjoy her game. He would likely figure out the rules before long.

"Have you ever been married?"

"I could tell you it's none of your business."

"I'm sorry."

"But I won't. Yes, I was married. She was an ICU nurse and we were married in my fourth year of medical school. Unfortunately, we didn't survive my year of internship."

"What was her name?"

"Elaine. She's married to a urologist now, has been for the past seven years. She's got a couple of kids and lives in Omaha."

"She divorced you?"

Elliot grinned at the disbelief in her voice. "Seems impossible, doesn't it?"

Her eyes narrowed. "Do you have disagreeable habits or something?"

"Do you mean do I believe in wife beating?"

"Nothing that extreme. Surely you weren't all that perfect though."

"I snore, but I don't believe that particularly bothered Elaine. I was young, George, and very intense, determined to be the best. One changes, thank God."

"Oh."

"You still have about fifteen questions left."

"I don't mean to be nosy, precisely," she said with disarming candor, "but I do want to get to know you. You're not at all boring, I think."

"Thank you," he said dryly. "Are you ready?"

She shot him a quick look that said volumes. Did her men have to pass some sort of test before she hopped into bed with them? He shook away the thought. There was something in her eyes that didn't fit. Well, he wasn't a horny kid anymore, and was quite willing to bide his time.

He walked her to her car. "Would you like me to follow you home?"

"No! I mean—"

"You've got an early call tomorrow."

"Precisely," she said with great relief, if not honesty.

"George, before I let you get away again, would you give me your address and phone number?"

She nodded, delved into her purse and wrote on the back of a business card. "Here," she said, smiling up at him.

"Thank you." At least now, he thought, he was a step up on Dr. Randy Hansen. She thrust out her hand, and he ignored it. He leaned down, not touching her, and lightly kissed her mouth.

"Good night, George," he said, and walked away.

She stared after him for a moment, words trembling in her throat. She wanted him to come back and kiss her again. Instead, she climbed into Esmerelda and drove thoughtfully home.

Chapter 4

He didn't call for a week and a half.

George had just turned the key in her front door when she heard the peal of her phone. "Come on, you dumb thing," she grated at the hapless key. She had just finished jogging two miles and was still breathing hard when she got to the phone on the fourth ring.

"Hello?"

"Hello, George," came a voice she had been waiting a week and a half to hear. "You sound like you've just run the marathon."

"Only two miles of it," George said, easing down into the hard-backed chair next to the phone.

"You jog?"

"Yes."

"I haven't seen you at the pool. You'll never beat me by Christmas at this rate."

George stared into the phone. "I've been swimming in the mornings," she said.

"Why?"

George wanted to be calm, to show him that she was sophisticated and knew how to handle men. Instead, she blurted out, "How can you be so damned obtuse? I've done nothing but chase you! If you thought I was going to keep throwing myself at you, you're—" She broke off at his deep laugh. "What," she demanded, clutching the phone all the harder, "is so funny?"

"I've got a couple of tickets to the symphony tomorrow night. Are you free?"

"I will have to check my calendar," George said coldly. She ruffled the telephone pages, then said, "Yes."

Elliot, the master hunter, smiled. "Excellent. Would you mind picking me up? The car's with my friendly mechanic. About seven?"

"All right. What should I wear?"

"Something long. Don't be late, George."

"I am never late," she said, and heard him chuckle.

She sat for a moment after she replaced the receiver. I think, she said out loud to the picture of a cat on the wall in the hallway, that I've just been had. She dialed Randy and left a message that she couldn't make their pizza date for the following evening.

Elliot was brushing the sleeve of his black tux when he heard the doorbell ring at precisely seven o'clock. He trotted downstairs, his eyes alight with anticipation.

He had expected her to look beautiful; after all, it was her stock in trade, as she had once blithely informed him. But still, he was silent a moment, looking at her. She was wearing a long, pale-green gown made of a soft, shimmery material that fell straight to the floor. It was sleeveless and shoulderless, held up by a thin cord of the same material that went around her throat and fastened between her breasts. He hair was piled on top of her head in something like a Gibson-girl style, with loose tendrils curling about her face and down her neck. She wore tiny diamond earrings and a glittering diamond pendant, and was carrying a black shawl over her arm.

"Come in, George," he said finally. "You look...very nice."

To George, it was a fine compliment. "Thank you." Her eyes twinkled as they swept over his black tux and pristine white shirt. "You look pretty good yourself."

"Thank you, ma'am. Come into my humble abode."

"Not so humble," George observed, gazing beyond the large entrance hall toward the elegant staircase.

"I've done a lot of work on the house. Come on into the living room."

The old Victorian was beautifully restored, even to the stained-glass windows, dark walnut wainscoting and beamed ceilings. She followed him through what she thought of as a receiving room, perhaps the room that had been used to hand out Christmas presents to long ago servants.

"I'm beginning to feel cheap, plastic and modern," George said as she gazed around the octagonal living room. The ceilings were twelve feet high, with carved cherubs grinning down at her from the molding.

Elliot grinned at her. "It's quite a showplace. I spend most of my time upstairs where I can be a slob if I want to. There's a comfortable master bedroom and another huge room I call a den. It's still got all the original built-in bookshelves and Oriental wallpaper, and a fireplace where you could roast a pig. Come to the kitchen and I'll fix you a drink."

"Do you have Perrier? I don't drink."

"Weight reasons? Religious reasons?"

"No. I'm a health nut, actually."

"Good. You'll probably be jogging when you're ninety."

The kitchen, unlike the rest of the first floor, was so modern it squeaked. A butcher-block table stood in the center, surrounded by stainless-steel appliances and counters.

"A concession to my housekeeper," Elliot said. He opened a well-stocked refrigerator, pulled out a bottle of Perrier and looked around for an opener. "Mildred keeps moving things around," he said, opening one drawer and then another.

When the opener was finally located, George said, "Now I feel better. That opener, at least, looks to be straight from the hardware store. And delightfully cheap."

He smiled and poured himself a glass of wine. "To our evening, George," he toasted her. "It's good to see you again."

She frowned at him over the rim of her glass. "You, I think, are a cruel person."

"I?" A thick black brow arched a good half-inch upward. She saw that his eyes were laughing a her. "Whatever do you mean?"

But George was losing herself in his eyes, leaf green, with gold flecks. "I'm sorry. What did you say?" Her voice sounded oddly breathless even to her own ears, and she flushed.

"Why do you think I'm cruel?"

"You're out of my league," she said simply.

"Really? You, a sophisticated model? I doubt it."

"Shouldn't we be going?"

Elliot nodded. "I wouldn't want to be late for Mahler," he said dryly. "We won't be besieged by folks wanting your autograph, will we?"

"No," George said. "It's too soon."

He waited for her to continue, but she said nothing more. He found himself a bit peeved at her reticence; that, or the sense of mystery about her. He couldn't decide which.

George fell asleep during the second half of the symphony, her head resting lightly on Elliot's shoulder. Her soft hair tickled his neck, and he could feel her breast soft against his arm. He had no desire to fall asleep, nor did he hear the music. He gently lifted her hand and placed it in his lap. She was becoming an enigma, and he disliked the thought. She had about as much guile as a five-year-old, at least that was the way she had seemed this evening. Or perhaps, he thought, she was out of his league, not the other way around.

When the applause broke out around them, George blinked and jerked upright. "Oh dear! Is it over?"

He squeezed her hand. "Did you have sweet dreams?"

"I hope I didn't snore," she said.

"Not loud enough to disturb our neighbors."

He helped her adjust her shawl, resting his hand on her bare shoulder for a moment. He felt her stiffen, then lean toward him.

"George," he said, and jerked his hand away. "Any place but here," he muttered under his breath. He was not in her league, he decided.

In the lobby, they were waved down by Dr. David Thornton and his wife, Doris. Elliot performed the introductions.

"You were at the picnic," Doris announced suddenly. "You were the one who won the volleyball game for us."

"And destroyed my sunglasses and my ego," Elliot said.

"I might sleep at the symphony, but never at a volleyball game!" George retorted, and gave him her dazzling smile.

"You look familiar," Doris continued, staring at George. "I don't mean to be pushy, but—"

David laughed. "You are pushy, my pet. We're going to Ivy's for a late dinner. Would you like to join us?"

Elliot looked down at George. "Do you have an early call tomorrow?"

George nodded regretfully. "I'm on the 6:00 A.M. plane for Los Angeles. I'm sorry. Weekdays are usually a problem."

Doris suddenly beamed. "I know who you are. You're the model, aren't you?"

"Yes," George said calmly. "And sometimes, like tonight, I truly regret it."

They made a date for dinner the following week. "She is unbelievably glamorous, isn't she?" Doris asked her husband as they walked toward their car.

"Oh, I don't know," David said, grinning down at this wife's pixie face. "What's a beautiful face and a gorgeous body?"

"Jerk," Doris said.

George parked Esmerelda in front of Elliot's house. "Would you like me to walk you to the door?" she asked lightly.

"Yes," he said.

"They seem like very nice people," George said.

"Yes," Elliot said again. "Will you be home tomorrow night?"

"Unfortunately, I won't be back until Friday afternoon."

Elliot turned to face her. He didn't give a damn about teasing her now. What he wanted was to make love to her until both of them collapsed. "I want to see you Friday night. All right?"

"Yes. I—I would like that."

He lightly touched his fingers to her cheek. "Come here, George," he said. He closed his hands over her shoulders and drew her into his arms.

George felt nervous, shy and exhilarated all at the same time. He merely held her against the length of his body, his mouth so close to hers that she could feel his warm breath.

"Please kiss me," she said, stretching up on her tiptoes.

Elliot looked down at her pursed lips and her closed eyes. He drew her tightly against him and lowered his mouth to hers. He felt her jump, as if surprised. Her lips were soft and giving, and very slowly he let his tongue trace over them, gently probing. When she finally parted her lips, his only thought was that he wanted her, wanted her more than he had ever wanted a woman. Suddenly, she seemed to yield to him, threw her arms around his neck and returned his kiss with fervent enthusiasm.

His hands strayed down her back to her hips. He caressed her, feeling her softness through the thin gown, and gently lifted her, pressing her against him. A moan broke from her throat, and he released her abruptly. He wanted an entire night with her, not just a couple of hours. It was as simple as that.

George swayed against him, and it was he who calmed her. "Friday night," he whispered against her temple.

"I—I feel odd," George gasped.

"I know, so do I," he said, stroking the nape of her neck. "Let me walk you to Esmerelda."

He opened the driver's side, but George made no move to get in the car.

She looked up at him hungrily. "Please," she whispered.

He kissed her again, quickly, almost roughly.

"Friday night," he said, and firmly pushed her away from him.

He watched her back out of the driveway and pause a moment in the street, her head cradled against the steering wheel. He felt shaken himself; it pleased him that she felt the same way.

George stood in the middle of her bedroom, shaking her head. "Damn, damn, damn," she said over and over, as if that would change anything. She yanked a long-sleeved, full-skirted black dress from her closet. Black fit her mood; she was in mourning, damn it! She fastened a gold chain around her throat and clasped a gold belt around her waist.

"You were born under the wrong star," she told her image in the mirror. She brushed her hair back from her face and jabbed in two gold combs. She'd had half a mind to call Elliot and tell him she was still in Los Angeles, but had chickened out. She wanted desperately to see him, despite...despite everything! Well, she thought, giving her hair a final pat, at least you couldn't tell from looking at her that the evening had ended before it started.

He arrived punctually and looked so damned gorgeous in a dark black suit that she cursed again under her breath.

"Your turn to see my house," she said, trying for a smile. "It's not as elegant and sophisticated as yours."

"I like it," Elliot announced, but he was looking at her. Her living room was long and rather narrow, furnished with rattan and an assortment of modern paintings and prints. A very comfortable-looking sofa faced a fireplace. A long bar separated a small breakfast parlor from the kitchen. She trotted him through the three bedrooms, one of them a study. Her bedroom was done in white wicker, and dominated by a king-size bed. He tried not to gaze too fondly at it.

"I like the hardwood floors," he said, wondering why she was rushing him about.

He helped her on with a soft black velvet cape. "Hungry?"

She smiled rather wanly. "Yes."

"We're going to Sausalito, to Ondine's. It's clear tonight, so we should have a great view."

She nodded and followed him silently to the Jaguar. Plush, she thought, fingering the soft light-gray leather seat. It suited him; elegant and subtle, not brash and overexuberant and loud, like Esmerelda. Like her.

They drove toward the Golden Gate Bridge, George staring out her window. Elliot gathered her hand into his and felt her stiffen. He did not release her.

"Tell me about Los Angeles," he said calmly. He could practically hear her sigh of relief, and he frowned slightly.

"It was rather insane, actually," she said, turning in her seat to face his profile. "Ben, Clyde and I—"

"Ben is your agent or manager?"

"Both, a longtime friend. We've been together since the beginning. Clyde's my photographer." She drew a deep breath. "Have you heard of the cosmetics firm, Braden-Tyrol?"

"Certainly. Are you going to model for them?"

"It's more than that," she said, regaining some of her excitement. "They've got a West Coast head-quarters in Los Angeles, and Ben and I met with their PR vice-president from New York to discuss the ad agency's schemes. It will involve a lot more than just modeling, Elliot. Have you ever seen the *Charlie* campaign on TV?"

Elliot nodded.

"Well," George said, drawing a deep breath, "I've signed a three-year contract with them. I'm going to be *Georgina* —they like my own name—and in about a month my face, for better or for worse, is going to be on TV, on billboards and in magazines."

"Good God," Elliot said, turning to her in astonished surprise. "You're a damned celebrity, George! Congratulations. I promise you the best champagne Ondine's stocks."

"Thank you. Unfortunately, I'll be doing more traveling than I would like. At least the ad agency wants most of the filming in this country."

Elliot asked her more questions, his voice warm and interested, and George felt herself grow more despondent, her replies becoming clipped. She was over her excitement and had spent so much time imagining this evening. Damn it, she thought, hunching her shoulders, she should have canceled, pleaded a terminal illness!

Elliot turned smoothly at the Sausalito exit. "I'll be in Boston next week," he said. "A conference."

She caught her breath. "When?"

There was a forlorn catch in her voice, and Elliot smiled. "Sunday to next Thursday."

"That's fine," she assured him. "I'll be in Dallas, meeting with the brass in their southwestern headquarters."

Elliot pulled the Jaguar into the parking area in front of Ondine's.

"Good evening, Doctor," the attendant said as he opened Elliot's door.

"You come here often?" George asked as he helped her out of the car.

"Now and then," he replied.

Their table, next to the southern windows that faced toward San Francisco, was ready for them. Elliot ordered a bottle of Dom Perignon from the hovering French waiter, then cocked an eyebrow at George.

"Will you have a glass? To celebrate?"

"Yes," she said.

Elliot sat back in his chair and studied her. She was toying with the bread sticks, her eyes on her plate.

"I had hoped," he said softly, smiling at her, "that we would be celebrating several things this evening."

Her head jerked up, and he saw a stricken look in her eyes.

Slowly, he opened his hand, palm up, on the table. "Give me your hand, George."

She placed her fingers lightly over his.

"I enjoy touching you," he said, gently stroking her fingers. Again, she seemed to withdraw from him. He remembered quite clearly the feel of her against him, the softness of her beautiful mouth and her interest when he kissed her.

"Won't you tell me what's troubling you, George?"

Think of something, you idiot! Thankfully, the champagne arrived. The cork was expertly popped and their glasses filled.

"To your success," Elliot said, and clinked his glass to hers. George took a couple of sips and set her glass down on the white tablecloth.

"Thank you," she said in a small voice.

"Do you like pheasant? They do it quite nicely here."

She nodded, not caring if she ate cardboard at the moment. She listened to him order and realized that she had to excuse herself.

She stayed in the women's room for a good ten minutes, then finally forced herself to return to their table.

Elliot took in her pale face and wondered what the devil was going on in her mind. She wouldn't look at him.

"George," he said, "You are acting strangely and I want to know why. What's the matter?"

"I—I'm very tired," she said.

He studied her face for a moment, then said gently, "You don't ever have to lie to me, you know."

She did feel tired, tired and angry. "I don't lie," she said. She met his eyes and blinked, as if dazed. All she had to do was look at him and she felt like wobbly Jell-O. She saw the gleam of satisfaction in his eyes and cursed herself for a fool.

"What else don't you do?" he asked suddenly.

"I don't stay in Los Angeles when I should," she retorted, without thinking.

Elliot smiled. She was nervous about going to bed with him, and he was pleased. It meant that she was not perhaps quite the experienced lover he had believed. His smile slowly flattened. That, or she was changing the rules of the game with him, now playing the tease.

"George," he said in an amused voice, "just because I buy you dinner, it doesn't mean that I expect payment in bed."

Her eyes widened, and she choked on the bread stick.

"Now, if you buy dinner, I expect the same courtesy."

"You don't understand," she blurted out, "I can't!"

"Can't what, buy my dinner?"

"I want you to stop laughting at me!"

"Ah," he said, looking away from her, "here's our dinner, at least the first course. Tell me how you met Dr. Hansen."

She shot him a smile and he wondered if Dr. Hansen wasn't a lover after all.

"He saved me from getting mugged in Central Park." She giggled. "Actually, there were two of them. I was pretty good at judo and at least Randy looks strong. The two guys decided we weren't good mugging candidates and took off.''

"Dr. Hansen was in medical school at the time?"

"Yes, in his fourth year."

"What the hell were you doing alone in Central Park?"

"Jogging."

"Even in Golden Gate Park you shouldn't jog alone. Okay?"

George felt both surprised and pleased at his concern. Maybe, just maybe, he would forgive her for tonight. She forked a small shrimp from her salad into her mouth. "I promise," she said.

"You went to Columbia, didn't you?" she asked him after a moment.

"Yes, and interned at Presbyterian."

"Tell me about it," she said, leaning toward him. "Some of Randy's stories are enough to curdle your blood."

Elliot was happy to oblige her, and the dinner passed pleasantly enough with reminiscences of the most hellish year in Elliot's life.

He still had her laughing on their way back to San Francisco with a story about a wino who had stripped in the emergency room and started to relieve himself in the drinking fountain.

When her house came into view, George clammed up. Elliot pretended not to notice. He turned into her driveway and switched off the motor. He made no move toward her, nor did he get out of the car.

"George," he said quietly after a strained moment, "I'm not going to attack you. Is that what you're worried about?"

"Yes—no, well, not really."

"That was a very definitive statement. I feel clear about everything now."

I'm worried about...other things."

"Good. I'm relieved. Would you like to stay here a minute and neck?"

To his amusement, she glanced at him warily.

"Really, George, I'm much too old to make love in the front seat of a car."

She knew she should hop out of the car now and retreat with some dignity, but she made the grave error of looking directly at his face.

"You have bedroom eyes," she said stupidly, unconsciously lifting her hand toward his face.

"You needn't worry, then. I'll close my eyes."

"I don't want you to think that I'm...well, that I'm—"

"A tease? It hadn't crossed my mind. Would you rather talk a while?"

"No."

He reached out his hand and picked up a curl of hair that fell over her shoulder. It felt soft and warm. "Do you dye your hair?"

"Of course not!"

"Well," he said, smiling wolfishly, "there is a way to prove it."

"How? Checking my roots every month?"

He groaned. "One of these days or nights, I'm going to figure you out, Georgina Hathaway." He gave her hair a gentle tug and she leaned toward him.

"Oh," she said when her mouth was an inch away from his.

His eyes gleamed in amusement. Very gently, he kissed the corner of her mouth, glided over her cheek,

then nipped the tip of her nose. The gearshift was between them, but for the moment Elliot forgot about it.
He slid his hand up under her hair and gently began to
knead the back of her neck. "You're tense," he said,
and pulled her face forward to his shoulder.

"No," she whispered against his shoulder, "I'm
stupid."

"Don't you plan to ever say something I expect?"

George arched her back to look at him, pressing her
breasts against his chest. "Please kiss me," she said
staring at his mouth.

Cupping her face between his hands, he caressed her
lips, slowly deepening his kiss until he felt the warmth
of her mouth and tongue. He felt her response but
maintained a firm hold on himself. He kept his hands
on her hair and her face, though he wanted nothing
more than to fell the rest of her in his hands. When he
released her, she was breathing hard.

"You been jogging, lady?"

His voice was softly teasing, and George, abruptly
shoved back into the present, buried her face against
his white shirt. Her hands, closed into fists, pressed
against his shoulders.

Elliot didn't understand her. Very slowly, he slipped
his hand between them and pressed his palm against
her heart. It was pounding. She was in worse shape
than he was, he thought, somewhat dazed. To his
surprise, she pulled away from him.

"I want to go in now," she said, gulping.

He smiled at her bowed head, though it was an effort. "As I said, George, one of these days—or
nights—I'm going to understand you. Come on,
lady."

He opened the car door and bounded out. For several moments, he concentrated on slowing his pulse.

"I'm too old for this," he muttered between deep breaths. When he turned back, George was already halfway to her door.

She looked strangely bereft. He decided he really was too old for games. He took her hand in his and shook it. "Good night, George. I had an...interesting evening."

She flinched, as if he had struck her. Jesus Christ, he thought, I'm playing the lead in a damned play and I have no idea what my lines are.

"Congratulations again," he said.

"Thank you," came the tense reply.

He stared down at her thoughtfully. "I'd like to see you again. Next Friday?"

Her face lit up like a Christmas tree.

"Oh yes, I'll be back from Dallas by then."

"Good." He lightly patted her cheek. "I'll call you. We'll have dinner with David and Doris."

What the hell, he thought as he backed out of her driveway, she was charming company, in spite of the bizarre game she was playing with him.

Chapter 5

It was George's first visit to Dallas, and she found it too hot, too flat and overwhelmingly friendly. She was feted at cocktail parties, swimming parties, press interviews and even a Texas barbecue, all as *Georgina*, the new Braden-Tyrol beauty girl. She was treated by most of the men as the valuable property she was, until after they'd had a couple of drinks. Then they seemed to think it was open season on George. She found it difficult sometimes to keep her dazzling smile in place.

She thought about Elliot, usually when she was lying in bed at night trying to sleep. She wondered if the Boston women were making it open season on him. She sent him a postcard of a Texas oil well. She breathed a huge sigh of relief when her plane finally took off from the Dallas/Ft. Worth airport.

"You did good, kid," Ben said, and perfunctorily patted her arm. "Take it easy for a while. You don't have anything to do until next Tuesday."

"The Texas hospitality was a bit overpowering," she said. "I only wish you had stuck around a bit more to help me fight some of it off."

"You did fine on your own. You're supposed to be a party girl, George." He continued over her disgusted snort, "What about Damien in New York? Owner of a fancy nightclub, a handsome dog, gobs of money. You spend all your time with him when you're there."

"Oh, Damien. He's good cover. I'll tell you a secret if you swear to keep your mouth shut."

"Let me order a drink first."

Ben downed half his Scotch before arching a bush eyebrow at her. "Well?"

"Ben, have you ever considered having an eyebrow transplant to your head?"

"Shove it, George. Now, what's this secret?"

"Forget it. I've decided to keep my mouth shut." It was just as well that Ben thought her something of a swinger. She was just plain tired, or else she wouldn't have been tempted to tell him that Damien Whyte was gay. Talk about good cover. They were made for each other!

"Women," Ben snorted, gulping down the rest of his Scotch. "Even you, George, can be a big pain in the butt."

"Thanks," she said dryly, and leaned back and closed her eyes. She saw Elliot, smiling in that beguiling way of his, his incredible green eyes caressing her face, and wondered if he thought about her, just a little bit.

"Good morning, Elliot," Lisa Dickerson said, looking up at her boss. "Welcome back. How was Boston? Did the conference go well?"

"Everything was fine. Any bombs drop while I was gone?"

"No more than usual. Dr. Baines wants one of the residents strung up by his heels, Dr. Luthor is growling about a promotion and the building committee needs your comments on the new wing."

Elliot grunted and walked into his office.

Lisa followed him after a couple of minutes with a cup of black coffee. "You haven't forgotten the fund-raising banquet tonight, have you?"

Elliot stared at her for a moment. "Damn," he muttered. He swilled down his coffee and slammed the cup on his desk. "Yes, I had forgotten. In fact, I made other plans. Any way out of it?"

Lisa shook her head, guessing his other plans included Georgina Hathaway. "Sorry, Elliot." She made a great fuss straightening a pile of papers. "You could, I suppose, take Miss Hathaway with you."

Elliot shot her a sharp look. "Actually," he said blandly, "I was supposed to have dinner with David and Doris Thornton." He didn't mention that George was the fourth.

"Oh," Lisa said. "Well, that's too bad," she continued, adopting his bland tone. "With her present, all those old crusts would probably drool in their cocktails."

"I would likely be spared making a boring speech."

Lisa shrugged elaborately. "Very true. Their respect for you would soar. Just think, the chairman of Radiology, a swinger!"

"I hear the phone, Lisa," Elliot said.

The morning was hectic. He resolutely put George out of his mind, canceled dinner with the Thorntons, wrote out his talk for the fund-raising dinner, met with Doctors Buzby, Daniels and Corby, and by one o'clock wanted nothing more than to swim fifty laps and collapse in the sauna. When he returned to his office, Lisa had gone to lunch. He sorted through the phone messages and mail on her desk. On top of the pile was a postcard of a Texas oil well. He smiled as he read George's sloping handwriting. He had tried to call her, but there had been no answer.

At three-thirty that afternoon, he closed his office door and dialed George's phone number.

He let it ring a half-dozen times. Finally, to his relief, he heard her exuberant voice. "Hello."

"George, this is Elliot. I've been trying to reach you."

"I was over at the stadium with Tod. He's got a new girlfriend and wanted me to check her out. Did you like Boston?"

"Enough. I just got your postcard. Did you enjoy Dallas?"

"It was a lot of hard work."

"And a lot of parties, I read."

"There always are. Tell me about Boston. I haven't been back in a couple of years."

"I'll tell you when I see you. I've got to cancel out tonight, George. There's a fund-raiser that I forgot about, and I'm the speaker. Sorry, but I can't get out of it."

"Oh."

Elliot had never heard such disappointment in one simple word. He smiled into the phone. "Will you cook dinner for me Saturday night?"

There was dead silence on the line. That's right, George, he thought, no more games like last weekend. For whatever reason, you've been chasing me long enough.

George was thinking frantically. She didn't know how to cook.

"It's okay, George. Forget it!"

"Seven-thirty," she said firmly. "Please dress comfortably."

"If you're sure..."

"Very sure. Elliot?"

"Yes?"

"Don't be late, will you?"

He grinned into the phone. "No, I won't be late."

"I'll pick you up if you're worried about the Jaguar konking out on you."

"Don't be impertinent, George."

He heard her laugh, and the sound brought a smile to his lips.

"See you Saturday."

He hung up the phone, swiveled in his chair and gazed out over the bay. The fog was rolling in and within a few minutes would blanket his view in white. He picked up the postcard and pictured George as she had appeared at the residents' picnic, her hair in a floppy ponytail, dressed in her Beau Jangles shirt and cutoffs. She had looked about sixteen. No, not sixteen, he thought, remembering those long legs. He drew a deep breath and quickly pulled his speech for the evening from beneath a pile of papers on his desk.

George stared down at the salad with its romaine lettuce leaves flopping over the sides of the bowl. How could the bloody thing have wilted so quickly?

She glanced at the clock. Where the devil was Marty with the white clam sauce and broccoli hollandaise? The front doorbell rang and she scampered to answer it. To her chagrin, Elliot stood there, fifteen minutes early, a bottle of wine under his arm.

"Hello, George. I live so far away, I didn't want to take the chance of being late and spoiling your dinner."

"Hi," she managed, her eyes darting up and down the street. All she needed was to have Marty pull up in front of Elliot with their dinner, like some sort of delivery service.

Elliot didn't notice her distraction. He was wondering how she could look more beautiful every time he saw her. She was wearing a pair of dark blue corduroy pants, a white silk blouse and no shoes. Her hair was loose over her shoulders, pulled back from her face with barrettes.

"I can't smell what you're cooking. I brought red wine. Will that be all right?"

To his surprise, George flushed. "Red wine is perfect. Actually, I...made everything earlier, that's why there are no yummy odors. Please, come in!"

"Can I help you with something?"

"Oh no! I want you to relax. You're my guest." She resolutely pulled the bottle of wine away from him and stayed on his heels until he eased down onto the sofa.

He stared after her as she trotted toward the kitchen, clutching the bottle of wine in her hand like a club. "George," he called, "are you all right? No fever? No chills?"

She appeared in the doorway, smiling frantically. At that moment, she heard Marty's car pull into the driveway. "Elliot, please come here a moment."

He rose, his head cocked to one side.

"I want you to see my...books! Here, in the study!"

She was dancing about, and Elliot decided to be amused and play along. "I would love to see your books," he said dryly. She practically shoved him into the small study and closed the door behind him.

She managed to reach the front door before Marty, her hands full, had a chance to ring. "Thank God you're here! Quick, Marty. My friend arrived early, of all things!"

Marty Taylor, a gourmet cook and a miniature whirlwind, as George affectionately called her, heaved a heavy casserole dish into George's hands. "I'll be in and out like a flash," she whispered. "Not to worry."

Heavenly smells of garlic bread and clam sauce floated through the air.

"George, don't forget to *taste* the spaghetti. About nine minutes, no more. You want it al dente." With those words, Marty giggled, gave George a quick squeeze and was out the front door.

When George returned to the study, she found Elliot seated at her desk, a novel in his hands. "Fascinating," he said. "I'm delighted that you allowed me to see your books."

She gazed at him warily. "Would you care to open the wine now? Dinner will be ready as soon as the spaghetti's done."

"Smells great," Elliot said, sniffing as he followed her into the kitchen.

"I'm heating eveything up. Elliot, would you like to check the spaghetti to see if it's al dente?"

"My pleasure." She watched him deftly twirl a strand around a fork, touch it to his finger, then taste it. "Nearly there."

He turned to her. "Good to see you, George," he said, and kissed her lightly on her mouth. Without shoes, she came to his chin. He slipped his hands beneath her hair and gently kneaded the nape of her neck. "Tension again, George," he said, his fingers caressing her.

"Clam sauce," she said, unable to keep herself from pressing against the length of him. "It always makes me tense."

He kissed her again. When his tongue gently probed her mouth, he felt her start, then snuggle closer against him, her arms going around his back.

"The spaghetti, damn it."

"The...spaghetti," she repeated stupidly, slowly stepping back from him.

Elliot willed his enthusiastic body to calm. He quickly turned away from her and drained the spaghetti. She had covered the circular butcher block table with a checkered tablecloth and had set a thick red candle on it. "Quite authentic," he said over his shoulder. He made her a wine spritzer, three-quarters soda with just enough wine to color it a pale red.

"Looks and smells great," he said once all the food was on the table. George sipped her spritzer and said, as if surprised, "This isn't half bad. Needs a little lemon to be perfect!

He told her about Boston, about the scull he'd taken out on the Charles. "I was on the crew at Yale. Lord, I didn't remember how much work it was."

George told him a bit about Dallas. "Imagine, they barbecued an entire cow! I didn't want to see it cooking, so I hid in the bathroom."

Elliot forked down another bit of the delicious clam sauce. He smiled to himself, then said blandly, "I like your use of cumin in the sauce, George. It gives it that snappy flavor. How much do you use?''

Cumin! What the dickens was cumin? "Oh, a couple of...well, not too much. You don't want to overdo."

"True. And the Parmesan on the garlic bread. Delicious. Did you grate it yourself?"

"No, I'm too lazy to do that."

"Sure tastes fresh. You're quite a gourmet cook."

"Thank you."

"You must give me your recipe for the hollandaise sauce. It was very creamy and not too cheesy. You must have spent hours stirring it."

"Oh, not hours," George said airily. "Save room for dessert, Elliot. I made cherries jubilee."

"It'll have to be later, George. You've stuffed me."

Elliot took a last bite of garlic bread and rose. He kissed her lightly on the top of her head. "You've worked so hard. I'll clean up. Why don't you go watch TV or...read a book?"

"Oh, no! You're my guest. How about brandy or a cup of espresso?"

"Coffee would be fine."

Elliot stacked the dishes in the dishwasher while George fiddled with the coffeemaker. "Need any help?" he asked, circling his arms around her waist.

He felt her muscles stiffen and spread his fingers over her. "You're very slender," he said, kissing her temple. His hands strayed upward. George leaned back against him, her eyes closed. His hands stopped. "Coffee's ready," he said, and released her.

He saw the stunned look on her face and smiled to himself. Men could tease, too.

George felt flushed, and she knew he knew it. She fumbled with the coffee cups, her whole body feeling taut and very warm. She managed a crooked smile.

"Would you like to watch TV?"

"If you like," Elliot said.

George carried the coffee cups into the living room and set them on the low table beside the sofa. She dropped to her knees and flipped on the TV. "I had cable installed last week. Let's check it out." Actually, she couldn't have cared less about any stupid movie. Her fingers suddenly froze on the dial. It was Chanel 31, the erotic movie channel. She sat back on her heels, staring. "Good grief, George," she heard Elliot laugh behind her.

On the screen, in full color, lay a naked man and woman, the man positioned between the woman's legs, his hands and mouth on her breast.

"Shall I turn it?"

Elliot grinned at her high, squeaky voice. Evidently she hadn't planned this at all.

"Not yet," he said easily. "Come here."

George crawled back to the sofa and sat cross-legged on the floor, between Elliot's legs.

"I ordered all the channels," she said, her eyes fastened on the screen.

"So I see. Now that is a position that much appeals to me."

The man's head was buried between the woman's thighs.

"Oh," George gasped. She scurried forward and switched off the TV. She couldn't look at him, not with a crimson face, not after what he had said, not when she was picturing him, naked, over her.

"Come here and let me take care of the tension...in your neck."

Her head shot up, but his expression seemed perfectly serious.

George settled herself once again between his legs and closed her eyes. She felt his firm fingers lightly massage her scalp through her hair, unfasten the barrettes and slowly move downward to her neck and shoulders.

"George."

She leaned her head back and opened her eyes to look at him upside down above her.

"You don't put cumin in clam sauce."

She blinked hazily, unable for the moment to grasp what he was saying. She felt his hands resting lightly on her shoulders, his fingers splayed downward. She arched her back, sending his hands lower.

"And the garlic bread...it was fresh Parmesan."

"I—I must have forgotten," she said, all her concentration on his hands.

He raised his hands and she felt him slowly unfastening the small buttons on her blouse. She heard his sharp intake of breath when he parted the material.

She wore no bra. Her breasts were creamy white, high and firm, her nipples a velvet dark pink. Very slowly, he stroked his hands downward along her sides.

"When you were sleeping at the symphony," he said softly, "I could feel you against my arm." He lightly caressed the sides of her breasts. "I wanted to rip your dress off and attack you."

His hands came around and cupped her breasts. George drew in a shuddering breath at his touch. He released her suddenly, clasped her under the arms and drew her onto his lap. She stared up at him, her back arched against his arm. "If it feels like this," she said hoarsely, "I wouldn't have minded at all."

He smiled, his eyes wandering slowly from her face to her upthrust breasts. "You are remarkably...nice looking," he said. He touched his fingertip to her nipple and she lurched upward to him. He gently pushed her back against his arm and lowered his mouth to hers. She tasted so soft and warm, he thought crazily, deepening his kiss. Elliot had never before been in a hurry to make love, at least not since he was a kid. But with George... He felt himself shudder when her lips parted and her tongue tentatively touched his. He stroked her breasts, letting his fingers memorize the feel of her soft flesh. He felt her hand tugging at his hair to bring him closer, heard her moan softly into his mouth as she arched upward against his hand. He gently pressed her onto her back and lightly ran his tongue over her nipple, nipping at her, caressing her until she squirmed.

His hand was pulling at the button on her jeans, jerking down the zipper. His fingers slipped beneath the band of her panties and rested a moment on her soft stomach. He stopped, pulling his hand back.

"George," he said, his voice raspy and deep, "I don't want to make love to you on a damned couch." His mouth trailed over her breasts to her throat and finally to her face. He gazed down into her eyes.

"You're awfully big," George managed, her fingers tightening about his shoulders.

"There's that, too." He grinned.

George shook her head and pulled herself up. She cleared her throat and blinked. "I'll go get into something more comfortable."

"That's right out of a 1940s movie," he teased her, winding his fingers through her tousled hair. "I'd prefer more of a caveman approach."

He stood and hauled her into his arms. "What are you going to do?" she managed.

"I'm going to take your jeans off and love you very thoroughly, every inch of you."

"Oh. Can't I take my own jeans off?" Wouldn't it be more sexy, more seductive, she thought hazily, if she were to put on her frothy peach negligee and glide slowly into the bedroom where he would be watching and waiting for her?

"How about mine instead?" He laid her on her back on her bed. "Just treat me, George, like you do the animals at the petting zoo."

She giggled. "Off with these things, lady," she heard him say as he pulled the jeans over her hips. She felt the cool air on her body and shivered slightly.

"That is cute, George. Green knee socks and panties that must weigh a good quarter of an ounce."

She was embarrassed suddenly. He was joking and teasing her and not consuming her in the throes of passion. Lovemaking was supposed to be serious business, with no thought to knee socks, for God's sake. She cocked an eyebrow at him. "I always wear knee socks at home."

"Leave them on. They're sexy. But not the panties," he added with a mock frown. She felt him slip them down over her hips, and she closed her eyes.

Elliot only looked at her. He didn't touch her, not yet. He rose slowly to his feet, his fingers on the buttons of his shirt. "Do you have any idea," he said, his voice so low that it sounded gravelly to his own ears, "how exquisite you are?"

"It's the knee socks," she said nervously, turning slightly away from him.

"No, George, don't hide from me." He studied her, knowing that once he lay down beside her, touching her, he'd lose all sense. "You don't dye your hair," he said, visually savoring the dark blond curls that covered her.

Her eyes flew open, and her hands flew downward to cover herself. "I told you I didn't." Her voice fell into a croak. He'd pulled his shirt off and tossed it to the floor. He walked to her favorite chair and sat down to take off his shoes and socks.

"Elliot," she said.

"Yes?" he said, not looking up.

She pulled the cover over her. "There's something I've got to tell you."

He pulled off a sock and tossed it toward a discarded shoe.

"You're a spy and you're sleeping with me to get state secrets for the government."

"No. Worse."

The other sock off, Elliot rose and unfastened his belt. "You're going to admit that you didn't make our dinner."

"I was going to admit that later!" She sucked in her breath as he stepped out of his jeans and underwear and stood marvelously naked, smiling at her. "Remember, just another furry beast from the petting zoo."

He started toward her, and George shrieked out, "It's the first time!"

Elliot stopped and tilted his head to one side in question. "You've never been to the zoo? First time for what?"

"I'm a...virgin. It's my first time."

Elliot simply stared at her. "George, how old are you?"

"Twenty-three."

"And you're a bloody virgin? George, only a woman who's lived in a convent or is a sexual neurotic is a damned virgin at twenty-three!"

"I've been busy," she said defensively. "And it's not that I don't know anything...I've done lots of kissing and stuff, just never, well, you know, *it*!"

Elliot sank back down in the chair. "You're a model, a playgirl," he said.

"Everyone thinks models are playgirls," George said in some disgust. "I don't want to be a playgirl, Elliot, but I'm awfully tired of being a virgin. That's why I—"

His head snapped up. "That's why you what?"

"Well, at the residents' picnic, when I saw you, I decided you'd be perfect."

Elliot dropped his head into his hands and said in a muffled voice, "A sex object. Christ, I'm nothing but a sex object to you."

George bounded from the bed, forgetting for the moment that she was naked. She fell to her knees beside him and clutched at his arm. "No, it wasn't like that, I promise! If you were a sex object, I would have seduced you right away, but I wanted to get to know you. Really, Elliot!"

He raised his head, and George saw that he was laughing, laughing at her.

"You...jerk! This is serious!"

He reached out his hand and lightly stroked her hair. "You are so funny. Why me, George?"

"You're the most perfect man I've ever met," she said simply. "And you're so beautiful and sexy. I thought that since you were older, and more experienced, you would make everything...well, easier and more pleasant."

"Well," Elliot said thoughtfully, leaning back in the chair, "I certainly didn't expect this when I came to dinner."

"You—you don't want me?"

He sat quickly forward at the forlorn question, studying her face. "Even a blind man would want you. It's just...Are you certain, George?"

"Yes. Elliot, really, I do know what to do." She gazed at him pointedly. He didn't look quite as...enthusiastic as before, but still..."You're awfully big. It won't hurt, will it?"

His laugh rumbled from deep in his chest.

"You're a doctor," she said sharply. "You must know these things!"

"No, sweetheart, it won't hurt, at least not much. Maidenheads are out, ever since little girls discovered baseball, volleyball and horses. It depends on how small you are."

"Oh," she murmured, flushing. "I'm twenty-three. I can't be that small anymore."

He smiled at her naivete. "Likely you're not," he agreed gravely.

George raised her head. "Can we...get it over with now?"

"You've convinced me." He rose, pulling her to her feet with him. George closed her eyes and stepped against him. It was a pleasurable shock to her to feel his manhood, now thoroughly aroused, pressed against her stomach. "Oh my," she whispered, "you feel so different from me."

Elliot was on the point of scooping her in his arms when he froze. "George, what are you using for birth control?"

She leaned back against his arms to look up into his face. "Well, nothing really. I-I didn't think about it."

He moaned. "I don't happen to carry contraceptives around with me." He had known that he would be making love with her tonight, but it hadn't occurred to him that a sophisticated woman like George... Well, it was time to revise all that nonsensical thinking. Damn and blast!

"We can't take the chance, George," he said in the saddest voice she'd ever heard. "The last thing you need is an unwanted pregnancy. You're a model, remember?"

"But it's only one time," she wailed.

Not likely, Elliot thought wryly. "Sweetheart, when was your last period?"

He saw that she was embarrassed and quickly explained, "You can't get pregnant unless the timing is right."

"Last week," she said in a muffled voice against his chest.

He rubbed his jaw against the top of her head. "Wanna make love?"

George gave him a dazzling smile. "Oh yes, Elliot, thank you."

He laughed, lifted her off the floor and carried her back to bed.

"Tonight will be all right," he said, gathering her against the length of him on the bed.

"How about tomorrow?"

He would have said no, but George pressed her stomach hard against him. "Maybe, but George, you've got to go to the doctor and get some protection. Or I can use something."

"No, I think those things men use are crass. Can't you do it? You're a doctor."

"You want a gynecologist. No pills. I'll make you an appointment with Margaret Smith for Monday."

"Okay," she said, and kissed his chin.

I don't believe this, Elliot thought, shaking his head. He wanted to give her pleasure, but it was a tall order, considering his own state. Slowly, he pressed her onto her back. "Lie still," he said softly. "And don't be afraid."

"With you?" she said softly, raising her hand to stroke his jaw. "I could never be afraid with anyone who plays volleyball as well as you do."

He smiled distractedly. Go slowly, very slowly, he repeated to himself. He kissed her, teasing her by resting his hand on her ribs, no higher and no lower. He felt the response in her, tentative at first, then natural and giving. He stroked his tongue over her soft mouth, and thrust it into her, a symbolic act that made her quiver.

"You are so soft," he whispered into her mouth. "Unbelievable for such a jock." His hand cupped her breast and he felt her heartbeat quicken.

"Can I touch you, Elliot?" she gasped when his mouth nibbled at her throat.

"Be my guest," he said aloud, wondering if he could control himself if she did.

Her hands roved down his back. "No," he said abruptly, "don't touch me, at least not yet."

"You don't like it?"

"I like it too much. Now hush." He leaned over her and gently took her nipple into his mouth. His hand inched down to her stomach and rested there a moment. He wanted to kiss every inch of her, but he was concerned that she would freeze up on him in embarrassment. Very slowly, his fingers tangled in the soft curls between her thighs. She grew very still.

He pulled himself back up on his elbow and gazed down into her face. "It's me, remember?" His fingers found her and slowly he began to caress her.

George stared up at him, a question in her eyes. "Move your hips against my fingers," he said, his voice thick.

She started to say she didn't know how, but her hips were moving. Suddenly, she felt a tremor that spread through her belly down to the tips of her toes. She gasped aloud.

"That's not so bad, is it?" he said, and kissed her. He felt her thighs go slack. Slowly, he explored her, gently easing his finger into her. He swallowed convulsively. She was moist, ready for him, and very small. He began to caress her rhythmically again, using all his wiles to bring her pleasure. She was moaning softly, her slender body pressed up against him, her fingers digging into his shoulders.

Suddenly, George cried out, lurching up. She stared at him in astonished surprise. She felt her body tensing, tight as a bowstring.

"Elliot!" she cried out almost frantically.

His fingers stopped, and she jerked upward. He pulled her hard against him and began caressing her again with his fingers. She was trembling, writhing against him. She threw back her head and cried out.

He watched her eyes flicker in mute astonishment as her body exploded with pleasure.

"That's it," he said softly.

She felt waves of pleasure, almost painful in intensity. Suddenly his fingers were gone from her, leaving her still awash with their sensation.

Elliot's body was throbbing, and he forced himself to take deep breaths. She looked so delicate, so exquisitely female. "George," he croaked. "Lie still." Slowly, he eased inside her. He felt her stretching, her muscles convulsing around him. She stiffened at the sudden discomfort. She grasped his arms, wanting him to stop.

"Relax," he said, forcing a smile. He wanted her so much, he felt as if his body was about to explode. "Just a bit more, George."

She gasped, but didn't move.

He knew he was hurting her. Better to get it over with, quickly. He drew back, then thrust deep within her. She sobbed softly.

"No more, sweetheart," he said, easing down over her. "You all right?"

"Yes." She looked at him thoughtfully. "I can feel you throbbing inside me."

"Jesus," he moaned. "George, damn it!" He pulled back and thrust again, unable to control himself. He felt as if he were shattering, and thrust until he was drained, his mind thankfully blurred. He fell forward, his head beside hers on the pillow.

George encircled him with her arms, lightly stroking his back. He was heavy on top of her, but she was far too happy to worry about it.

Elliot was able finally to ease himself up on his elbows. He lightly kissed the tip of her nose. "That wasn't bad, was it?".

"Oh no," she said, but she was frowning.

"What's the matter, George?"

She looked up into the depths of his incredible green eyes, struggling for words to express her feelings. "You're inside of me. You're part of me. I just never imagined anything like that. It's like we're one person."

He wanted to laugh, to retort with a teasing comment, but he couldn't. He kissed her instead, demandingly this time, forcing her lips to part to him. He felt her arms tighten about him, and drew back, breathing heavily.

"Next time," he said roughly, "I won't hurt you."

He rolled onto his side, bringing her with him. "That," he said, "was better than dinner."

"That was dessert."

"No cherries jubilee?"

"They're from my friendly baker." She sighed against his chest. "I doubt I could have convinced you that I made them."

"Next time, George," he said, smiling against her cheek, "we'll make clam sauce together."

"No cumin?"

"No cumin," he repeated, laughing.

"Good grief," George suddenly exclaimed, rearing up on her elbows. "It's nearly midnight!"

"I trust you had fun while time was flying."

"For the most part," she said primly, though her eyes were twinkling. "Elliot, I've never slept with a man before. I mean...*slept*. Would you stay with me tonight?"

"If you promise not to snore like you did at the symphony."

"Just don't start humming Mahler."

Elliot kissed her again and leaned over to snap off the lamp.

"This is nice," George said, sighing contentment as she snuggled against him.

"Very nice," Elliot agreed.

Chapter 6

George awoke slowly, not wanting to be pulled from the unbelievable dream. It was a soft moan from deep in her throat that made her blink in the darkness.

"Elliot," she whispered, wrapping her arms around his shoulders.

"I hope I'll be just as pleasant as that dream, George," Elliot said, shifting his body over her.

"You were the dream, but this is better." She pressed his head down and felt his mouth caress her temple, her nose and finally capture her mouth. She felt him hard against her and incredibly hot against her belly, and moaned with the pleasure of it.

She tried to shift beneath him, to open herself to him, but he raised himself on his elbows, holding her still.

"Not yet," he said softly.

She could make out the planes and shadows of his face now in the sliver of moonlight from the window, and the dark thick lashes that veiled his eyes. "Why not yet?" she gasped, her hips pressing upward with no instruction from him.

"You just woke up."

"You, Dr. Mallory, don't know what I was dreaming!"

"I have a good idea, since I was providing the action."

"You mean...your fingers really were...that is, you were..." She blushed and buried her face against his chest. Elliot smiled and nuzzled her throat. "You are so delightful, George."

His light teasing tone brought her head up. "How can you make fun of me when I want you to..."

"You aren't finishing your sentences, George."

"I want you to love me!"

"That's what I want, too. May I?"

"I don't think I know any other word except yes where you're concerned."

He eased down her body, kissing and stroking her. His warm mouth was on her stomach, his tongue tracing a hot trail lower over her skin, to where she felt a fierce insistent ache. When he finally caressed her, she froze in embarrassment and pulled away with a loud gasp. "You—you can't do that!"

"Am I going to have to put you back to sleep?" The deep huskiness in his voice made her quiver in response. "That's better," he murmured, pressing her back.

George swallowed, holding herself rigid. When his mouth closed over her, she felt a scalding heat that made her legs stiffen. His hands slipped beneath her hips and lifted her, molding her against him. She thought she would break into a thousand pieces if he stopped.

Elliot felt her resistance vanish, and he reveled in the sensuous feel of her, the taste of her. When he felt her body begin to stiffen, he quickly rose and eased inside her. He gasped at the pulsing warmth of her, and held himself rigid, trying to gain control of himself.

"Elliot," she whispered brokenly, "please."

He thrust deep inside her, his fingers rhythmically caressing her as his own passion mounted. Suddenly, she cried out, her nails digging into his shoulders, and he felt the small warmth of her closing tightly around him as her body shuddered. He felt himself exploding and her cries mingled with his own.

He lay on top of her, gently smoothing back her tangled hair, calming her and himself.

"Oh, goodness," George managed when her breath slowed.

"Indeed," Elliot said, his voice rough with surprise.

"I think this could become addictive."

He raised his head and smiled into her dazed eyes. "Have I created a monster?"

"You were the one who woke me," she protested, busily tangling her fingers in the hair on his chest.

"Am I too heavy for you, George?"

"No. Please don't go." She slipped her arms around his back and sighed in contentment.

He kissed her lightly, nuzzling her lips with his. Suddenly, he stopped. He began to laugh, unable to help himself. "Oh, lord, what a fool I was. Now I understand!"

"Stop that, Elliot! You're leaving me!" She could see his devilish grin and frowned at him. "What do you understand?" she demanded.

"Last weekend. I wanted to make love to you and couldn't figure out why you were acting so strange. I thought you were being a tease, and I wanted to throttle you." He began to laugh again, shaking his head at himself.

"It wasn't my fault," George muttered in a sulky voice.

"No, and now it's funny, but believe me, it wasn't last weekend. I was in sad shape, George. Why didn't you simply tell me it was your period?"

"Do you have to be so direct? Can't some things be left unsaid?"

"Probably. But in the future, don't feel you can't tell me things. All right?"

The future. Unknowningly, George gave him a dazzling sweet, utterly contented smile. "Okay," she agreed sleepily.

Elliot stared down at her. What the hell had he meant by the *the future*? He felt tired and sated, and he said something his mind hadn't approved. He pulled George against him and closed his eyes. He'd worry about it tomorrow.

Bright sunlight poured through the windows, but it was the aroma of fresh coffee that made George's nose twitch and her eyes open. Memories of the previous night coursed through her mind, and she smiled and stretched languidly.

"You look like a contented cat."

Elliot was walking toward the bed, carrying a tray with two cups of steaming coffee, wearing only his pants.

"You look as delicious as the coffee smells," she said, pulling herself upright.

Elliot's eyes fell to her breasts, and he frowned slightly as he felt his body responding. "Cover yourself up, woman, or the coffee will freeze over before you get to drink it."

She flushed at his intimate gaze and pulled the covers to her shoulders. "Nobody has ever brought me coffee in bed before," she said for want of anything better.

Elliot grinned. "That I know for a fact."

He settled beside her, and raised his cup. "A toast," he said, "to a woman who looks beautiful even after a night of debauchery."

George sipped her coffee. "Elliot," she said, cocking her head at him. "Do I look...different now?"

"Yes," he said after a moment in a soft, teasing voice. "You look unutterably smug and pleased with yourself." His voice roughened. "George, the cover is slipping."

She gave him a saucy smile. "Your chest is uncovered." She reached out her hand to stroke him, but he drew back.

"No, sweetheart. You need a little time. You're probably sore."

"Why do you call me sweetheart?" she asked a bit breathlessly.

His eyes darkened, as if he were displeased with himself.

"You called me sweetheart last night, too."

"Well," he said at last with a crooked grin, "there's no way to shorten George. Consider it your nickname."

"Oh," she said somewhat disappointed.

He rose and stretched. "Drink your coffee while I take a shower. Then we're going sailing. And no, George, I refuse to shower with you, at least this morning."

"Coward," she called after him.

"You're right!" He laughed and disappeared into the bathroom.

She was a bit sore, she discovered later when she was showering by herself. How did he know, anyway? Maybe, she thought sourly, she wasn't the first virgin who had seduced him.

Elliot wasn't a bit surprised to find George an excellent sailor, quite at home on his Islander Thirty-six. She teased him about the name, *Paradox*.

"David was being clever," Elliot said as he steered closer into the wind. "We own the boat together, thus *pair of docs*."

She finished winching in the jib and sat back to let the sun warm her face. "I've been thinking about buying a sailboat," she said in a perfectly serious voice, "but I'm concerned about the ongoing costs. I haven't figured out how to make it a tax write-off."

Elliot almost laughed. She looked so damned beautiful, the wind swirling her honey-colored hair around her face, and so damned young. "David and I lease it out to a sailing instructor during the week. We can write off about eighty percent.

"Now why," George said in disgust, "didn't I think of that?"

"I gather you have had other things on your mind the last month," he teased her.

"True," George allowed, taking the wheel from him, "and now that I've gotten what I wanted, my poor brain can return to more important projects. I want to head for Angel Island, sailor. Prepare to come about!"

The afternoon became quickly overcast and George shivered despite her two bulky sweaters.

"Let's tie up at Sam's for lunch, then call it a day," Elliot said. He cocked an eyebrow at her. "For a woman," he drawled, "you ain't a bad sailor, except for that luffing job."

George only laughed at him. "I seem to remember, big mouth, you saying something of the sort at the volleyball game last summer. Seems you had to eat your words then."

"Come swimming with me tomorrow, twit, and we'll complete your humiliation."

"One of these days, doctor, I'm going to have the last word!"

"I should live so long" he grinned, ruffling her hair.

"No," Elliot said firmly, pulling her arms from about his neck, "I'm not coming in. Believe me, it's not that I don't want to, George, but we aren't going to take the chance." He kissed her, and stepped back with great nobility.

"I'll call you in the morning after I've got an appointment for you with Dr. Smith."

She looked like a child who had been deprived of a coveted present. He lightly touched his fingertips to her cheek. "I'll see you tomorrow, George," he said.

Elliot picked up the phone. "Dr. Mallory."

"Elliot? Maggie Smith here. Since you were the referring... physician, I thought I'd let you know about our patient."

He should have known, damn it! "I'm certain you handled everything quite professionally, Maggie. Now, if you don't mind—"

"Oh, no, Elliot! It's quite professional that I get back to...the primary-care physician."

She's really enjoying herself, Elliot thought, grimacing into the phone.

Maggie had a look of unholy glee on her face. It was all she could do to keep from laughing. "Now, Elliot," she said, clearing her voice, "I'm glad to report that Miss Hathaway is in superb physical condition; indeed, I don't think I've ever seen a woman who was quite so...superb."

"Maggie," Elliot growled.

"Sorry, I didn't mean to digress. I asked Miss Hathaway all the usual questions. When I asked her if she's sexually active, she gave me a radiant smile and assured me that—just a moment, let me quote her exact words—here we are: 'Oh yes, Dr. Smith, now that I know what it's all about, I plan to be very active.'"

"Thank you for being so thorough," Elliot said sarcastically. "Now, if you're quite through, Maggie, I've got—"

"Not quite through yet, doctor. Just for the—*your* record, Miss Hathaway is rather small. But she is so healthy, I doubt if she'll have too much difficulty having children."

"Maggie!"

"I did so much enjoy this referral, Elliot. Miss Hathaway is such a delightful young woman. It is a pity, though." She paused, allowing a deep sigh.

"What's a pity?" Elliot asked, taking the bait.

"Well, as you know, we have fourth-year medical students rotating through. It's always up to the patient to decide whether or not the student can be present or perform part of the examination."

"Well?"

"John Elderbridge, the student, is still recovering, I fear. He took one look at Miss Hathaway and nearly swallowed his Adam's apple when she wouldn't let him in the examining room."

"Are you quite through now, Maggie?"

"John trapped her outside my office and asked her out. She gave him this impish smile—that was the way he described it to me once I pried it out of him—and told him that she planned to be much too busy for the next fifty years!"

Elliot ground his teeth.

Maggie couldn't prevent a giggle any longer. "I'll call you, Elliot, when I get the results of the Pap smear." She had gotten over her infatuation with Elliot Mallory some time ago, and could enjoy the situation to the fullest. Poor Elliot! His days were numbered.

George made seven laps, then collapsed in the shallow end of the pool. She felt Elliot's hands close about her waist and lift her out of the water.

She sat panting, then pulled off her bathing cap and goggles. "Skiing," she gasped. "There I've got you."

"Don't count on it," he said, tickling the bottoms of her her feet. "Now, while you're recovering and trying to find excuses for yourself, I'll finish my laps."

George went soft in the stomach at the sight of his back and muscled arms stroking gracefully through the water. At least, she thought, smiling contentedly, now she knew the cause and the cure.

He swam only twenty laps, then hoisted himself up beside her.

"Getting old?" she asked, grinning at him.

"Probably. What's your excuse?"

"Too much work," she said rather pensively while kicking her feet in the water. "I've got to go to New York tomorrow."

"When will you be back?"

"Flying back Saturday night, late. The first filming will be in Central Park, in one of the horse-drawn carriages."

"Since this is your last night in port, wanna spend it with me?"

George's eyes twinkled at him. "My, but you're easy!"

He groaned. "Lady, you don't know how close you are to being ravished, right here in front of Tim, the hulking lifeguard, and all the hospital staff."

Her eyes turned smoky as they traveled over his body. "George, for God's sake! I'd just as soon not embarrass myself here, of all places."

Elliot suddenly slipped back into the water, scowling up at George's laughing face.

"What did you think of Dr. Smith?" he asked in a rather offhand manner.

"She was charming, Elliot. We talked a lot, and she loves to laugh."

"I'll just bet she does," he muttered under his breath.

"It wasn't nearly as traumatic as I feared it would be. But would you believe it—there was a *male* medical student who wanted to be in the examining room!"

Elliot could only grin. "No kidding," he said in a bland voice. "What did you do?"

"Why I said no, of course."

He waited to see if she would mention that he'd asked her out, but she didn't. In fact, she was frowning slightly.

"What's the matter?"

George flushed. "Well, Dr. Smith told me it will take a little while to get the diaphragm. I really urged her to have it ready today."

"I suppose she laughed some more and agreed."

"How did you know?"

"Mind reading, George, and what's called professional courtesy. Come over to my place about six, okay? We'll barbecue something."

"I'd love to. What's your specialty?"

He winked at her. "It's called foreplay, George."

Elliot lay on his back, his body tense with anticipation. He kept looking toward the bathroom. "George," he called out after ten minutes, "did my hamburgers make you sick?"

"No, damn it!"

"What's the matter?"

He heard a wail and a crash.

He bounded to his feet and strode to the bathroom. He opened the door to see George, beautifully naked, standing in the middle of the bathroom, the diaphragm in her hand, and his electric shaver on the floor beside her. She looked up at him and grabbed for a towel.

"What's wrong, sweetheart?" he asked gently, knowing exactly what the problem was. It wasn't the time to tease her, though the situation was hilarious in the extreme.

"I can't get the damned thing in," she muttered between clenched teeth. She looked as though she were ready to sink through the floor in embarrassment.

He managed through great effort to keep the grin off his face. "I'll show you, okay?"

"Are you out of your mind?" She stared at him aghast. "How would you know anything about it? No, don't tell me how doctors know *everything*! I'll figure it out."

"Very well, I won't say anything of the sort. It's all right, George. It just takes a bit of getting used to, that's all."

"But lovemaking is supposed to be spontaneous, not this—" She waved the hapless contraceptive around angrily. "I feel like such a fool! Would you please remove yourself, Elliot?"

"I'll get the instructions for you," he said, and walked to the dresser. He handed the paper to her through the crack in the door. "Sure you don't want me to show you what to do?"

"Go climb in the trunk of your car," she said furiously, and slammed the door.

At least, he thought, he could grin, since she couldn't see his face.

When she finally walked into the bedroom, he gave her a lopsided smile, and said, "You ready to be spontaneous now, lady?"

"I'm so mortified," she muttered, her eyes fastened on his chin.

"You're not supposed to be embarrassed around doctors."

His voice cracked, and he couldn't contain the rumbling laughter any longer. George, her face beet red, grabbed a towel that was lying on a chair, and flicked it expertly on his thigh.

"You jerk!" she yelled at him. She readied the towel for another attack, but Elliot grabbed her around her waist and hauled her over his shoulder. He dropped her on her back on the bed, then fell on top of her, pulling her arms above her head.

He waited until she stopped struggling against him. "Now, what do you deserve for that slap on my leg?"

"I'll get you, you just wait!"

He looked down at her thoughtfully, but his eyes were laughing. "I've never thought it particularly wise for a little shrimp to go after the big shark. Retribution is certain." He grasped her wrists in one of his hands and came up to his knees, straddling her. "Now, lady," he said, running his fingers under her arm.

"No, Elliot," she gasped, trying to struggle free.

He began to tickle her in earnest. George tried to buck him off, gasping for breath, but it was no use.

"Tell me you're abjectly sorry," he said, raising his fingers for a moment.

"Sorry, my foot!" George yelled, kicking at his back.

His fingers descended again, and George was writhing, gasping in laughter, "Stop! Elliot, I can't stand it! I'm sorry."

"Abjectly sorry."

"All right, *abjectly* sorry!"

Elliot grinned down at her. Her face was red from her struggle, her eyes tearing from laughter, and her hair tangled about her head. She looked utterly beautiful. He eased down beside her, keeping her arms above her head, her wrists clasped in his hands.

"You'll never attack my body again? Let me rephrase that—no more attacks with a towel?"

"If you promise to stay out of the bathroom and not laugh at me anymore."

"More torture," Elliot murmured. He smoothed the silken hair from her forehead, dipped his face down and began to nibble gently on her lower lip. His tongue glided over her mouth, exploring its texture and outline while his hand roved down to her breasts.

"You are so perfect," she said, as if in wonder. He felt her hands stroking his belly. "I wish I had met you five years ago."

"If you had," he said roughly, "I would have been thrown in jail."

"Ah, no," she said, "I was eighteen then."

There were no more words between them. He loved her slowly, with exquisite care, and when she cried in pleasure, he felt as if his own small part of the universe was perfect. Then he was lost in the maelstrom of his own pleasure.

"Jesus," he groaned, his chest heaving with aftershocks, "that hasn't happened to me for years." He fell heavily on top of her.

"It was all the foreplay before, during and after dinner." She grinned, tightening her hold about his back. He raised his head and smiled ruefully down at her. "George, I think if I saw you in a snowstorm, I'd still want to fling you down and have my way with you.''

''Wanna go to Tahoe, sailor?''

He kissed her and George tasted herself on his lips. She found herself wondering what he would taste like.

''What are you thinking?''

She flushed slightly, unaware that her eyes had darkened at the thought.

''Come on, you promised not to hold anything back from me.''

''I was wondering how you would...taste.''

He stared at her an instant, then felt himself responding as if she had been loving him. ''I'm sorry I asked,'' he said in a ragged voice.

''And I am glad.'' George pressed upward, drawing him deeply into her.

He made love to her again, even more slowly this time, pacing both of them, until finally she buried her face into his throat and moaned her climax.

''How nice,'' he said, kissing her temple. But George was asleep.

When Elliot woke the next morning, George was gone. There was a note propped up by the coffeepot. ''I'll miss you. Beware the phantom towel. George.''

Chapter 7

The Saturday night air was damp and chilly, though the San Francisco fog did not reach as far south as the airport. Elliot steered the Jaguar smoothly into a parking space close to the airport elevators. The parking garage was as empty as it ever got; it was nearly midnight. He smiled to himself as he pictured George's surprise at seeing him. She had called him once from New York and they had made plans to go sailing on Sunday. He really hadn't intended to come pick her up, but the evening had seemed long and empty, as had the entire week.

He walked through the airport, checked the arrivals board and made his way to the gate. For once, the plane was on time. He stepped back as the passengers came into the waiting area, and paused a moment when he saw George, filling his eyes with her. Her hair was pulled away from her face and fastened with a clip at the back of her neck. She was wearing a burgundy wool pantsuit, every bit as expensive as her Gucci boots, and she wore no makeup. She raised her head slightly, shifting her carry-on bag, and he saw the shadows beneath her tired eyes. She looked unutterably weary. She nearly walked past him.

"George," he said softly.

She turned toward the sound of his voice. Her incredible violet eyes widened at the sight of him, and for a moment she stood very still and simply stared at him. Almost miraculously, all signs of weariness disappeared from her face. Her eyes brightened, and he felt shaken at the naked joy in her gaze. Despite himself, he felt a surge of possessiveness.

"Elliot!" She dropped her bag to the floor and flung herself into his arms. She laughed and hugged him, kissing his cheek, his nose, his chin, "What are you doing here? Oh, how marvelous! What a wonderful surprise!"

Elliot closed his arms more tightly around her and lifted her off the floor. For a long moment, he simply held her against him, breathing in the sweet scent of her hair, feeling the soft yielding of her body against him.

"A bloody long week, George," he said, and lowered his mouth to hers. He heard someone chuckle and drew back. Jesus, he thought, he was nearly thirty-eight years old, and here he was acting like a horny teenager in an airport! He made the mistake of looking into her eyes. No one, he thought, should have such expressive eyes. She was consuming him with that look, her longing so palpable that it stunned him. He patted her back awkwardly and leaned down to pick up her bag.

"Do you have luggage?" he asked.

"Yes, but only one bag," she said, her voice breathless. "The Braden-Tyrol folk provide my clothes for all the filming and even for my appearances. All I had to take was comfortable stuff, like jeans and my jogging shoes."

He tucked her hand into his. "You look tired, George."

"Perhaps, just a bit," she said, smiling up at him.

"We'll sleep in tomorrow," he said.

"I suppose your temperamental Jaguar is running tonight?" George asked, her eyes sparkling as she took a double step to keep stride with him.

"Don't be a smart ass, lady, not when I'm saving you twenty-five bucks in taxi fare."

She arched a perfect brow at him. "I'll just have to figure out a way to pay you back for all your trouble," she said blandly.

Later, at home, as he pulled her against him and gently stroked her back to calm her, he felt her breath becoming even again and felt her heartbeat slow against his chest. He realized he felt utterly calm, at peace with himself and the world. It was frightening, frightening as hell.

On the edge of sleep, George said vaguely, "I can't imagine still being alive after that. Will you always make me feel like I want to shout and cry and laugh all at the same time?"

Always. "Yes," he said, and pulled her more tightly against him. No knee socks tonight, Elliot thought inconsequentially, as he listened to her breathing even into sleep. Her panty hose lay in a pile by the bed, her expensive clothes scattered beside them. He felt her fingers curl in the hair on his chest as she burrowed her face into his shoulder.

"My houseplants," George said suddenly, coming half awake. "I hope Marty remembered to water them."

Elliot laughed. "Anyone who cooks as well as Marty wouldn't forget," he told her. "Maybe she's even planted some cumin for you."

"Jerk," George said vaguely, and promptly fell back into a deep dreamless sleep.

They wouldn't be sailing that day, Elliot thought, when he woke up near eight o'clock the next morning. Sheets of rain streaked down the bedroom windows. He sat up when he saw George emerge from the bathroom, wearing one of his huge beach towels.

She stopped a few feet away from the bed and smiled at him. "Even though your beard looks scratchy, I'll keep you."

Elliot ran his hand over his jaw. "I always have an eight o'clock shadow." He didn't touch the blanket that had fallen below his waist. "What are you doing up so early, George?"

"I'm going to make you a wonderful, high cholesterol breakfast, sir, since you are not only a very important person but also very sexy."

He groaned, remembering vividly her only attempt at an omelette. "George," he said, "how did you survive before you met me?"

"Well," she said, grinning angelically, "don't forget all the hot dogs and peanuts at the stadium."

Elliot threw back the covers, stood up and stretched. He could feel her staring at him, and it pleased him that she admired his body.

"Would you take a shower with me, Elliot? You never have before, you know."

"But you've already showered."

"I didn't use any soap."

"I have created a monster," Elliot said thought-fully, and lunged for her. He grabbed a corner of the towel, and she yelped and ran into the bathroom.

"Can I wash you?" George asked when they stood pressed together under the shower.

"Only at your own risk, sweetheart," he said.

"Is that a promise?" she whispered, kissing his chin.

Her soapy hands were wandering lazily down his chest. "Yes," he said.

George was thorough. She started with his hair, then moved slowly down his body, scrubbing every inch in her wake. "Damn it," he growled finally, "We're going to run out of hot water, George!"

She gave him an impish smile and slipped to her knees. She carressed him, as lightly as a butterfly's wings. He felt near to bursting when she finally reared back to rinse him. But still she didn't rise. He drew in his breath sharply, and waited.

The tentative touch of her lips on him was like a bolt of liquid lightning, and his fingers clutched her wet hair.

He felt her hands stroking his thighs, sweeping around to his buttocks. Suddenly, she released him, coughing, and sat back. "This is going to take a lot of practice." she said.

"Come here, you tease," he growled, and pulled her to her feet. He lifted her. "Wrap your legs around me, George," he said.

"Oh," George said as he eased inside her. "This is better than my fantasy," she whispered against his mouth.

But he knew he couldn't pleasure her like this.

"Before we drown, let's get out of here," he said. She laughed at the regret in his voice.

It was close to noon before they made omelettes. "Is this enough cholesterol for you, sweetheart?"

George eyed the beautiful creations regretfully. "Just a bit for me, Elliot. I've got to lose two pounds by next Wednesday."

"What!" he thundered at her. "God, George, I can see your ribs sticking out from here!"

"I know," she said calmly, "but television adds a good ten to fifteen pounds."

"So where are you going to lose it? Off your big toe?"

"My breasts are too big. Do you know that they had me wearing a special bra that flattened me?"

Elliot slapped some butter on his wheat toast. "Jesus," he said. "That's ridiculous."

"I know," she said in the same calm voice, "but it's my choice of careers and I must obey the rules. Ben thought it was funny, said his wife wouldn't be so jealous of me anymore once she saw me looking as flat in front as in back."

Elliot motioned irritably to the table. "Well, sit down and eat something."

"The funny thing is," she continued, shaking her head as she sat down, "and I tried to tell the ad men this, I can't lose weight off my bosom. It comes off everyplace else, but not there."

"You're bloody perfect just the way you are."

"And you, my lord very important person, are prejudiced."

"I am a bloody man, George, and I don't want you any skinnier." He thrust a piece of toast heaped with butter and honey at her. "Eat or it will be the worse for you."

She laughed and obligingly bit into the toast, mentally calculating the calories.

It stopped raining in the early afternoon and they went jogging on the beach near Seal Rock. George had a smooth gait, and Elliot discovered that she had no difficulty keeping up with him. They finally collapsed on a blanket Elliot had brought.

"Elliot," George said, staring out over the gray waters of the Pacific, "tell me about your accountant. I'm not pleased with mine at the moment. He gave me some rather stupid advice on a high-risk tax shelter—oil drilling in Oklahoma—and I lost the last of my respect for his ability."

"George," he said, laughter lurking in his voice, "I'm an old man who knows more about jogging than tax shelters."

"Come on, Elliot. I saw several prospectuses in your study, and I—"

"Aha," Elliot pounced. "You're worried that I'll lose my shirt!"

George had the grace to blush. "Well, it is something that I'm quite good at, really. I honestly thought I wasn't natural when I went to college. I was terrible in biology and English and history. Then, three years ago, when I was finally making more than enough money to survive, I dabbled in the stock market and with excellent results." She flipped over on her stomach and rested her chin in her hands. "The one prospectus you have on the limited partnership for condominiums in Santa Barbara, well, that one sounds interesting and bears some looking into. Would you like me to study it for you?"

For a moment, he only stared at her, remembering himself at twenty-three. He wouldn't have recognized a tax shelter if it had bitten him then. In fact, he wondered if tax shelters had even been invented then. He looked into her very serious and very beautiful face and said, "I suppose you've heard that doctors are notoriously naive with money?"

"Well," she said fairly, "doctors have other things to worry about, and I'll bet you were excellent in biology."

"Do you know how unusual you are, George? Other than your crazy name, that is."

She shrugged. "Everyone has different talents, and, of course, I won't be a model all my life. Who knows what I'll be doing after I'm thirty?"

"Maybe you'll be a madam at the Mustang Ranch."

"But," George shot back, her eyes twinkling, "madams can't have sex, can they? That, I never want to give up!"

He laughed and pulled her over against him. "Kiss me, madam," he said.

"Only if you promise to let me study that prospectus for you."

His eyes were on her soft mouth. "George," he said, smiling, "you can study anything you bloody well want to."

"Does that include you?"

"I am number one on the list."

She lowered her mouth, for the first time the aggressor. "You are so beautiful," she breathed, nipping at his lower lip, then lightly gliding her tongue over his mouth. He felt her thigh press lightly into his groin and realized for the first time that they were on a public beach.

"Damn," he muttered, and gently pushed her off him.

She slanted a provocative look at him and, without conscious thought, ran her tongue over her lips. He groaned, and jumped to his feet. "Come on, George, before I throw you down on the wet sand and ravish you."

"Come where?" she asked, rising to her knees.

"Home to bed, of course."

He sought to distract himself as they walked along the beach back toward the car.

"Tell me about your week in New York."

"Well, you'll be seeing my face on the tube, probably the end of this next week. It's only a short ad, but you wouldn't believe the hours that went into making it."

"Tell me about it. I know about as much about your work as you do mine."

"Up at 5:50 A.M. and into makeup and wardrobe by 6:30. You see, the makeup has to highlight the particular outfit I'll be wearing, and the wardrobe man and makeup man enjoy arguing endlessly about whether or not my eye shadow should be purple or green. Then it's usually sit around and wait for the technicians and the director to get their act together. In this case, the wretched horse in the ad simply wouldn't cooperate. And then it rained."

"And you evenings?" There was a slight edge to his voice that surprised him. Thankfully, George didn't seem to notice.

"Parties. And smiling and drinking Perrier until I feel like I'm going to float away. At least there's Damien."

"Who," Elliot asked carefully, "is Damien?"

"A dear friend who also happens to own a very popular nightclub. I've known him for years."

"George, you haven't lived for years!"

"Well, about four years, then. He helped me when I was first breaking in."

"But you never went to bed with him."

She gave a small, secret smile. She said only, "No, I was waiting for you, you see. Oh, I forgot. I told Tod about you. Don't be surprised if he shows up on your doorstep, unannounced, and asks you all sorts of crazy questions about your intentions toward me and all that."

"George, how old is this Damien?"

"Damien Whyte is his name, and he's about thirty, I guess. Why?"

"Just curious." But he wasn't; he was suddenly jealous and it appalled him.

"Elliot," George asked suddenly, her voice light and bland, "what do you think of marriage?"

"It's a necessary institution, I suppose," he said readily enough, though his thoughts were still whirling elsewhere.

"Was your first marriage very unhappy?"

"It's been a long time, George," he said, "and to be perfectly honest, I don't remember all of it now. There were quite a few fights and upheavals. Elaine was a very emotional woman. I don't mean that in a negative sense, at least not now. Perhaps then I did. I was so bloody tired most of the time, and so involved with medicine, that the last thing I ever wanted was to argue with my wife. In hindsight, I suppose I simply withdrew from her, not really caring what she thought or did. The final straw for Elaine was when she told me she was pregnant. I remember that I just stared at her, thinking about the enormous responsibility of a child. After I got over the shock, it was too late. She'd had an abortion.''

"I'm sorry," George said, fiercely delighted that this Elaine was far away.

"I was an ass, and I couldn't really blame her for walking out on me." He stopped suddenly. "God, I haven't thought about Elaine like that in years."

"Then," she said, scuffing the toes of her sneakers in the sand, "you aren't really against marriage."

"I like my life the way it is," he said.

She tucked her hand in the crook of his arm and gave him a winsome smile. "I do too."

"So what do you want me to say to your brother Tod?"

"Tell him that you're the sexiest man in town and his sister has great taste and chased you until you collapsed in defeat."

"The only time I've collapsed is with you under me!"

"Perhaps," George said with great seriousness, "you had better not get that specific with Tod. He's so funny. He's quite a playboy, but he expects me to be the cute little innocent sister."

"Well, you are cute and little." And you're all of twenty-three, he wanted to tell her. The fifteen years that separated them couldn't be erased. He knew she was infatuated with him. He was her first lover. At least she would never forget him. He said abruptly, "There's a Thanksgiving party next week. Will you be in town?"

She glanced at him in askance, but followed his lead. "Yes. Is it some kind of a doctors' party?"

He nodded. "It's rather a tradition with David and Doris. Yes, all doctors and their wives. Actually, there are a couple of women doctors and their husbands."

"And were you a *couple* in past years?"

He grinned at the sharpness in her voice. "Yes, but fickle as hell, never the same woman twice, except for Eileen. This year all the men will likely trample me in a stampede to get near you."

"Who is Eileen?"

"Eileen Raeburn, an attorney here in town. Smart lady."

"I see," George said. She lowered her lashes so he wouldn't see the jealousy in her eyes. "I look forward to seeing David and Doris again," she said. "You know what I'd like to do first?"

"Something noncontroversial, I hope."

"Oh yes. Since I'm going to meet all these doctors, I'd like to see them in their natural element first. I've only visited your office once, Elliot, but I've never seen your empire. Can I come and visit tomorrow?"

"Why not?"

He realized why not when he walked with George down the hospital corridor the following afternoon. Her casual jeans were gone, replaced with a gray wool dress, gray heels and elegant makeup. She looked as if she'd just stepped off a fashion page, utterly out of place in a hospital and too beautiful to be believed. It occurred to him that she had taken pains with her appearance to please him, to make him proud of her. He led her into his office first. "You remember Lisa Dickerson?"

"Oh yes," George said brightly. "Hello. It's nice to see you again."

"Miss Hathaway," Lisa said. "Dr. Mallory told us you would be visiting today. Everyone is anxious to meet you."

"I'm sure," Elliot said dryly. "Why don't we start with the Nuclear Medicine section first, George?"

He was aware of every medical student and every resident who passed them providently in the hall. Not to mention the techs and nurses who appeared around every corner. "Dr. Bainbridge," he said steadily, ignoring all the attention directed their way, "heads up the section. He looks as jolly and innocuous as Santa Claus, but he's a tough old bastard, and I'll bet he knows more about tax shelters than you do."

Dr. Bainbridge was at his most charming. "A pleasure, Miss Hathaway," he said, squeezing George's hand. He proceeded to introduce her to his staff and the residents on the service. He showed her the nuclear medicine equipment, all of which was Greek to George. But she was at her most bubbly and enthusiastic, and Elliot saw the looks that went from him to George and back again. He groaned inwardly. He wondered if he was going to be known as the dirty old man of the department.

"And here is the CT section. We call it the CT scanner, but the real terminology is cumputerized tomography. The machine has the ability to image through layers of tissue, and it's made radiologists important again. Here is Dr. Dole. I'll let her explain what she does to you."

Elliot realized when they were with Dr. Dole that George had a gift with people. She made them feel good, made them feel as if what they were saying was the most important thing in the world. They ran into Dr. Randy Hansen in Angiography.

"George!" Randy exclaimed, rising quickly. "What are you doing here?" He looked at Dr. Mallory and swallowed his Adam's apple.

"I'm getting the royal tour, Randy. Now, Elliot tells me that Angiography is a lot like surgery. You do procedures and cut people."

"I don't do much yet," Randy said. "Here is Dr. Kerlaw. He and Dr. Wallace and Dr. Prince are about the best on the West Coast."

Dr. Kerlaw, the only one of Randy's three heroes in the office, was a tall man in his early thirties with short black curly hair, dark eyes and a very bland expression. He shook George's hand and said in an unnerving monotone, "Actually, Randy lied. We're about the best on both coasts."

Elliot laughed. "We've no shortage of great doctors with great egos, George. But since Bob here went through our program, I'll have to go along with him. How's the wife, Bob?"

"Very pregnant," Dr. Kerlaw remarked. "Would you like to see one of our procedures?" he asked, turning to George.

"If it's like surgery, then there's blood. Right?"

"Just enough to make the decor interesting."

"Count me out," George said on a weak laugh.

On the way back to Elliot's office, George said, "I think Dr. Kerlaw has the most unaccountable sense of humor."

"True. You should see the three of them together. It's a circus, and there's no safety net."

It didn't occur to Elliot until some time later that all the heads of sections and most of the attending physicians had been in their offices. That was unusual. He smiled grimly. Lisa must have phoned every section, warning them that Dr. Mallory was bringing a very important guest around.

"Fascinating," George said, summing up her visit that evening. "I didn't know what to expect, you know. All of the doctors were so nice and so...chummy, not at all standoffish, or snobby. Thank you, Elliot. Next, sir, you're going to have to visit me on the set."

George, bless her innocence, Elliot thought, hadn't the foggiest notion that every doctor in radiology had wanted to meet her.

Chapter 8

Elliot pulled some socks from his dresser and smiled at the sight of a pair of George's bikini panties nestled in with his shorts. Her favorite knee socks, and his, too, were folded neatly by his housekeeper in with his. Red, white and blue striped. He imagined her naked, wearing only those socks, and wondered wryly when just the thought of her would cease making him as horny as a kid. The thought came unbidden into his mind that he didn't want to stop wanting her.

"Nothing like an old fool," he muttered to himself.

But the sight of George that evening was more potent than the thought of her. She met him at the front door wearing a floor-length, wool plaid skirt, topped with a lacy silk Victorian blouse. Her hair was piled on top of her head in the Gibson-girl fashion, with long tendrils curling lazily around her face. She looked utterly exquisite.

"Knee socks or panty hose?" he asked her.

"I always wear panty hose for formal occasions," she said, laughing at him. "My, Dr. Mallory, but you look charming tonight." Her eyes darkened, mirroring her thoughts, and Elliot quickly helped her on with a long wool cape and ushered her out to the car.

"I trust you're planning on stuffing yourself tonight. Doris puts on quite a feed for Thanksgiving."

"Oh, yes," George said cheerfully. "I lost three pounds and am quite ready to gain one back."

His hand, of its own will, reached over and lightly stroked over her breast. "Thank God, you still feel the same."

She giggled and moved closer to him, dropping her hand on his thigh. "Elliot," she said seriously, "when men lose weight, do they lose it...well, I mean... there?" Her fingers lightly glided over him.

"No," he choked, moving her hand quickly elsewhere. "I'm hungry and I don't want you to wreck us. Now, pick a subject and move your mind to loftier things."

Her idea of loftier things involved a discussion of a particular tax shelter in condominiums. He found himself asking her to explain terms that she used with the greatest ease. He was no longer surprised that she was so knowledgeable, just a bit dazed. A model and a Wall Street wizard. He didn't know whether to be intimidated.

David and Doris lived in St. Francis Wood, a comfortably elite section that George thought particularly un-San Francisco. No proud old Victorians, and all the houses detached with yards. Lights were blazing from both floors when they arrived. "I think from all the cars," Elliot said, helping her out, "that we're going to be making an entrance."

"Will you make me one of your famous wine spritzers," George asked, "so I won't feel like a sore thumb?"

"You got it, sweetheart. One teaspoon of wine in soda water."

"And a twist of lemon."

He was kissing her on the top of her nose when Doris opened the front door.

"Well," she said, giggling, "it's about time! George, how lovely you look tonight. Do come in, both of you."

The Davidsons' house was furnished with early American antiques. "Oh," George said, "hooked rugs! Campbell, aren't they? And an Adams lamp? How lovely, Doris!"

"Yes, yes, and thank you. We like it," Doris said comfortably, her eyes on Elliot's face. "Let me fetch David."

"Campbell rugs and Adams lamps? Is that something else you know about, George?"

George leaned closer to Elliot and said in a whisper, "Actually, I made up the names. Doris just went along with me. And, doctor, up until a very short time ago, there was a very big something I was totally ignorant about."

Elliot refused to be drawn in. "Are you referring to me specifically or the general subject of sex?"

George squeezed his arm, and said mournfully, "I thought I had you on that one."

"I'd head for the Neptune Society if I thought that would ever happen."

"Well, for your information, my mom's very much into early American. I couldn't help but absorb something."

"Here's our celebrity," David said, smiling widely at George. "You were on TV, George, just about two hours ago. I spotted you myself and promised Doris a bottle of that perfume you were pushing."

"Don't go that far, David," George said, laughing. "Although the stuff isn't that bad."

"Congratulations, George," Elliot said. "If Doris's dinner isn't up to snuff, I'll go watch TV with the kids and try to find you."

Suddenly, George wasn't smiling. "Please, David," she said quite seriously, "don't say anything to anybody. I'd just as soon not be gawked at."

"Okay, lady," David agreed. "Sorry I missed you last week when you were visiting the hospital. Why didn't you bring her around, Elliot?"

"Just Radiology. How did you know I was visiting, David?" George asked.

Elliot groaned, and David grinned. "George," he said, "everyone knows you were there. In fact," he added with a wolfish smile toward Elliot, "my male residents are still talking about you."

"David," Elliot said, interrupting him, "are you going to introduce George around, or do I have the pleasure?"

About fifteen minutes later, Elliot was standing by the fireplace with Dr. Paul Erikson, a gynecologist. Paul, a man of infinite good taste and dry wit, said to him in a bland voice, "Well, old man, it appears you finally understand my standards, at least in one area." He was looking toward George, who was standing in the center of a small group, laughing, then listening intently, all in all, a marvelous addition to the party. "Lovely girl. If only I were fifteen years younger and not so blasted married."

"I've thought something like that myself," Elliot said, with a long pull on his Scotch.

"Come on, Elliot, you're practically a spring chicken—rooster, rather. My, there's Eileen Raeburn, only this time she's with Alex Amery. She seems to be looking this way quite a bit, Elliot."

"Ah, the table looks about ready for us," Elliot said. "With any luck, Paul, you'll have the first course before you're called to deliver a baby."

"Age does have some privileges, Elliot," Paul said. "Only triplets could tear me away this evening."

Elliot excused himself and made his way to Eileen. He hadn't seen her since the previous summer, since before he had met George. "Hello, Eileen. You're looking lovely tonight."

Eileen Raeburn smiled and placed her hand in Elliot's for a moment. "I've missed you, Elliot," she said.

"It has been a while," Elliot said evenly. He nodded toward Dr. Amery. "Where did you meet Alex?"

"Actually, I handled his divorce. He's finally recovering, I think. What have you been up to?"

"This and that, you know, much the same as usual."

One of Eileen's eyebrows shot up. "Not from what I hear," she said, her gaze going for a moment toward George.

David's voice suddenly rang out over the noise. "Dinner is served. Everyone get in line."

Saved by the turkey, Elliot thought with a grin.

Dinner was a buffet on card tables set about the living room to accommodate the thirty-plus guests.

"Elliot," George said, savoring a big bite of dressing, "isn't that cumin I taste?"

"Doubtful," Elliot said. "It's usually found only in Mexican food. But try some fresh Parmesan."

Eileen Raeburn's stomach was in a jealous knot at a neighboring table. She said to Maggie Smith, "Elliot seems to be robbing the cradle, I see. Male menopause is hitting him early."

"Try the giblet dressing, Eileen," Maggie said. "It's delicious. Alex," she continued without pause, "was just telling me about his research grant. It's quite interesting."

After dinner, Elliot sat back watching George, amused at the few moments' doubt he had had about bringing her. She was the youngest person there, and he had thrown her willy-nilly into a group of doctors and spouses, most of them in their thirties and forties. He found himself wondering if he hadn't planned the evening as a sort of test for her. More fool he! At the moment she was listening to Mrs. Krantz talk about her needlepoint, her young children and how the two didn't go together very well. George was the very soul of interest. When Dr. Albert Krantz mentioned that George looked familiar to him, George said easily, "Perhaps. I smile a lot and push makeup and perfume. It's my job."

Mrs. Krantz promptly forgot about her needlepoint, and grilled George for a good ten minutes.

"George," Elliot finally broke in, "can I get you some more wine?"

"Why don't I come along and make myself a spritzer?" She excused herself charmingly. "Phew! Thanks for the rescue."

"You done good, sweetheart. You're something of a celebrity. You've got to expect people to be fascinated."

"I suppose so," she said on a small sigh.

"What is this? Don't you like all that attention?"

"Well, not really. I already know all about me. I like to talk about other things."

"Sometimes," Elliot said slowly, "I don't believe you're real."

He was speaking to Donald Harley, a GU radiologist, listening to the garrulous man with half an ear, when he saw Eileen make her way over to George. He cursed softly and excused himself. It was his intention to sidetrack Eileen when Doris caught him.

"No, Elliot," Doris said quietly, "let George deal with it. Does she know about Eileen?"

"I've mentioned her, but that's all."

Eileen had consumed four glasses of wine, but her legal mind was as clear as ever. "So," she said in her best lawyer's voice to Georgina Hathaway, "you're a model."

George turned friendly eyes to the woman and smiled, nodding.

"My name is Eileen Raeburn. I don't believe we've met."

George's smile did not slip. "I've heard you're an excellent lawyer. Have you practiced long in San Francisco?"

"Yes," Eileen said, her eyes glittering. "Law requires a lot of practice. There's very little flitting around. Have you been modeling long?"

"Since I was eighteen," George said agreeably.

"I understand that a model's working life doesn't last all that long. Beauty fades, and all that."

"Yes, that's true. I've always thought it a bit unfair. Female models must be flawless, which translates to very young, whereas male models can be forty. Ad agencies want the 'grainy' look in men, but it's out of the question in a woman. If I wanted to start modeling now, no one would pay me any mind. Most women start at eighteen, or even younger."

"I suppose it's wise of you to look to the future. A husband, now, that would be a reasonable thought, I suppose. A steady source of income in an uncertain future."

Gloves off, George thought, sighing to herself. "Models work very hard, Miss Raeburn, incredibly hard as a matter of fact."

Eileen shrugged elaborately. "Perhaps, but the first qualification is a very pretty face, isn't it?"

"Let us say an interesting face, one that photographs well. You, for example, would photograph quite dramatically, I think."

"I'm not a brainless blonde, Miss Hathaway."

"Eileen," Elliot said, interrupting smoothly, "I see you and George have been getting acquainted. Have you told her about that antitrust case you're working on?"

Things hadn't gone as Eileen had envisioned them. The wine was beginning to muddle her thinking, and here was Elliot asking her about that ridiculous case!

"Yes, Eileen," Dr. Amery, her escort for the evening, said pleasantly from behind Elliot's shoulder, "you haven't told me what you think is going to come of it."

"A disaster averted, and very smoothly, doctor," George whispered quietly to Elliot a few minutes later. "She's very nice, I think, but jealous. She doesn't like me at all."

"No, probably not."

"It is too bad," George said, looking toward Eileen Raeburn. "She is a good lawyer, isn't she?"

"One of the best," Elliot gravely assured her. "You're sure you're not brainless? All that blond hair..."

George slanted him an intense look, her eyes turning nearly voilet. "I lied to you," she whispered. "I'm wearing knee socks."

"Under a dress?" He looked skeptical.

"Yes. The ones with all the orange splotches against black."

"I can't handle the thought. Let's get out of here."

Chapter 9

Elliot had always enjoyed spending Christmas with his parents, his sister and brother-in-law and their three children in Connecticut. But staring out of his bedroom window onto the snow-coverd front lawn, he knew that this year was different. George was in England, of all places, shooting an ad for Braden-Tyrol in Warkwickshire, the backdrop of a medieval castle. He missed her, and the admission alarmed him. He smiled vacuously at his two nephews, who wouldn't have a prayer of finishing their snowman if they didn't stop arguing.

He looked down at a handsome new wristwatch, George's Christmas present to him. Engraved on the back were the words "To the only man in San Francisco." He wasn't quite sure just how she meant that. He grinned, remembering her response to his gift, a dozen pair of handknit knee socks, each with a design and colors more outrageous than the last. A muscle jumped in his cheek, for the thought continued to their last night together, her slender legs, covered to the knees in pink wool with black stars, wrapped around his flanks. He could feel himself inside her, all his, and his rational thoughts scattered like autumn leaves to the wind. It was that night he had agreed to spend the first week in February with her and her family in Aspen, skiing. "It's our yearly family get-together," she had told him, lightly kissing his ear. "Lots of skiing and lots of noise from all my nieces and nephews. There's five of them, all under seven years old. A real madhouse."

He knew he shouldn't meet her parents or her family. He was thirty-eight years old, and she was twenty-three. Nothing could change that. She would thank him, he told himself, for not taking advantage of her infatuation with him—at least, he amended silently, not more advantage than he had already taken. He could not allow himself to forget that, despite all her sophistication, she was still painfully young and in need of a man closer to her own age, a man of her own generation. And she was well on her way to being famous. She had an exciting life before her, and Elliot had no intention of curtailing it by making her his wife. It simply wouldn't be fair to her. February, he thought. He would speak to her in February. It was just so damned tough. She was out of town perhaps two weeks of every month, and seeing her after a week's absence was like a drink of water to a thirsting man. He couldn't seem to get enough of her, selfish as he knew he was being.

Just as she had visited him at the hospital, he had been with her at a shooting session in Monterey. Even though he had believed her when she told him she worked hard, he supposed he had still pictured her prancing about in lovely clothes, kissing a perfume bottle. But that afternoon on the wharf in Monterey, he had watched a group of at least a dozen thoroughly professional men and women orchestrate a thirty-second commercial. It had taken close to four hours. George had sat patiently as various artists fiddled with her face, her hair and her clothes. He could see the weariness begin to tell on her as it went on and on, but she didn't complain. During each take, a dazzling smile appeared on her face as she acted out the nuances the director called for. She was, he realized, as much a professional as the rest of them. He had seen her exhaustion and hadn't pressed to return to Carmel, to the Brittany Inn, where they had spent the previous night. She had fallen asleep almost immediately and had not awakened until they had finally reached San Francisco.

He suddenly jerked up the window and leaned out, shouting, "All right, Jeff! Cut it out! The raisins are for your snowman's eyes, not Mark's ears!"

Downstairs in the pine-scented living room, Mrs. Mallory was sipping a cup of coffee, listening with half an ear to her daughter's chatter.

"He is different, Mama, surely you've noticed! Why last night, Papa even beat him in chess, and you know that's unheard of!" She paused a moment, then drew a surprised breath. "My God," she said, smiling widely, "I bet it's a woman. My dear brother is in love!"

Mrs. Mallory regarded her garrulous daughter above the rim of her coffee cup. Lindy was a dear, but such a gossip. "My dear," she said at last, her voice as calm as a placid lake, "Elliot's divorce was over seven years ago. He's had ample time to find himself another wife. He hasn't shown the least bit of interest.''

"Then how do you explain his..." Lindy hesitated a moment, searching for the right word. "His lapses? Oh, he says all the right things, and puts up with the children's pranks like he always does, but his mind wanders. And he has a new watch,'' she added, as if clinching the matter. "When I commented on it and asked if I could see it, Elliot looked uncomfortable.''

"And refused? How odd, I asked him, too.''

"Speak of the devil!'' Lindy said brightly as Elliot walked into the room.

"Mother looks thoughtful,'' he said, cocking a black eyebrow at his sister. "So I presume you've been telling tales again, Lindy.''

"About you, brother!''

"Would you like some coffee, Elliot?''

"No, Mother, not just now. I thought I'd go out and save Mark from Jeff's sense of humor.''

"Would you like to leave me your watch, Elliot?'' Lindy asked. "You don't want to damage it in the snow.''

"Lindy,'' he said, "sometimes I wish you were five years old again and I could toss you in the garbage can.''

At least, Elliot thought later, dutifully admiring the snowman with his nephews, Lindy was easy to sidetrack. He had left her recounting several occasions in their childhood when he had mistreated her.

He didn't see George until the second week in January. After her England assignment, she had stopped in Michigan to visit with her parents. "You're lonely as hell, you stupid bastard," he finally admitted to himself, and felt immediately better.

But only until he realized it would be time to speak to her when she returned to San Francisco. He would insist that she start going out with other men, men her own age. How long would it take then? A month? Two? Theoretically he accepted it, but his guts churned at the thought of another man even kissing her. Then she came home, and all thought of it fled from his mind.

Elliot didn't know what woke him. One minute he was dreaming about racing a red Lamborghini in Italy, and the next he was sitting up in bed, fully awake. George wasn't beside him. He looked blankly at the clock: 3:00 A.M. He pushed off the covers and walked to the bathroom. She wasn't there. He switched on the bedroom light, looking for his robe. It wasn't there, either.

"George?" he called. There was only silence.

He felt a frisson of alarm run through him. He trotted downstairs, turning on lights as he went.

He stilled a moment in the dining room. Was that a moan he had heard? He quickly walked into the kitchen and turned on the light. At first all he saw was the glare from the appliances. His breath caught in his throat when he saw George. She was lying on the floor, pressed against the refrigerator, her body curled in the fetal position. Her hair tangled and loose, hiding her face.

"George?"

She raised her face, white and tearstained. Suddenly, her features twisted in pain and she drew her legs up against her chest, twisting away from him, pressing close to the refrigerator.

"What is it, George?" He dropped to his knees beside her and tried to gather her in his arms. He could feel her pain rippling through her, communicating itself to him. "For God's sake, what's wrong?" He pulled his robe aside, his first thought that she had appendicitis. She was wearing only a pair of panties, and he slipped his hand beneath them to feel her belly. She sat up in pain, panting, trying to push him away.

"Where is the pain?" He caught her face between his hands. "Where do you hurt?"

George couldn't speak for a moment, with the pain jabbing at her. She was trying not to scream. "It won't go away," she gasped. "It's always gone away before. It's worse this time."

He forced himself to calm. "Where, George?" He slipped his hand back to her belly and gently probed. "Here?"

"No, over there. Always there."

He eased her back on the kitchen floor and drew down her panties. "Show me," he instructed her in his professional voice.

Her fingers, as if frightened to touch her own body, hovered a moment, then flitted down. He probed lightly, and abruptly let go. Probably ovarian, he thought rapidly. "This has happened before? When?"

"The last two months," she panted, trying to pull her legs up to ease the pain. "It wasn't so bad, and it went away within hours."

"The same time of the month? Close to your period?"

George felt dulled with pain. Questions! Why was he asking her questions when all she wanted to do was die! "Yes."

He thought rapidly. She had finished her period only yesterday. He quickly pulled her panties back up and jerked his robe tightly around her.

"Don't move," he said. "I'll be back in just a minute and we'll go to the hospital."

Five minutes later, Elliot was galloping back into the kitchen, dressed in blue jeans and a pullover. He had never been so afraid in his life. He drew his robe about her and lifted her in his arms.

"It won't be long, sweetheart," he murmured to her as he carried her to the car.

There was no traffic, and he made it to the hospital in twelve minutes flat. He kept talking to her as he drove. "Just a few more minutes, sweetheart. Hang on. Just a few more minutes."

He screeched into the emergency parking lot. When he lifted her out of the car, she moaned, squirming against him to ease the pain. The night duty nurse looked at him and took in the situation quickly. She looked him in the eye, waiting.

"I'm Dr. Mallory. I need a nurse in an examining room quickly."

"Yes, doctor," she said, blinking.

The nurse met him at the entrance of one of the gynecology rooms. "We'll start with an IV, normal saline through a sixteen-gauge angiocath, draw routine preop bloods and an HLG. Tell the radiology resident to bring down an ultrasound unit. Leave me your stethoscope." He paused a moment, and added, "And bring in ten milligrams of morphine sulfate."

He cradled George in his arms, unwilling as yet to lower her onto the table. "Just a few more minutes," he said. "Then there'll be no more pain, George." He knew he shouldn't give her anything, not until he was certain what was wrong with her, but he couldn't stand her pain anymore.

He had her in an examining robe and had taken her blood pressure when the nurse raced back into the small room. "Hold still just a second, George. You're going to feel a needle in your arm." He quickly swabbed her arm and plunged the large needle into a vein. She didn't even feel it, he thought.

He nodded to the nurse. "Send this blood off, please. I'll call you in a minute."

He uncovered George again and started to press down on her belly, but she moaned in pain. He pulled his hand away and gave her a large dose of morphine, enough to make her groggy. He cradled her in his arms and rocked her back and forth. "In just a little while, George, there'll be no more pain." He waited perhaps another minute, then said, "Try to take deeper breaths, George. Is the pain lessening?" He could feel her beginning to relax. He felt her nod against his chest. "Deep breaths. That's it." He wanted to ask her why the hell she hadn't awakened him. And this was the third month of the pain. He felt her head loll against his arm.

"Is the pain gone?"

"Yes. I know it's there, but it feels like it's at a distance somehow, and I feel so sleepy."

Her eyes closed and she murmured, "I'm sorry, Elliot. Such a bother for you. I'm sorry."

"Don't be ridiculous," he gritted at her in a hoarse voice, but she seemed to be sleeping. He looked down at her peaceful face and smoothed the tangled hair behind her ears. He kissed her gently on her mouth, and called for the nurse. He wrote the emergency-room note himself and told the nurse that he didn't need an intern. While the radiology resident was setting up the ultrasound, he called David. It occurred to him only after the phone began ringing that Maggie was her gynecologist.

On the fourth ring, he heard Doris's sleepy voice. "Hello?"

"Doris, Elliot. I'm sorry to wake you, but I've got to speak to David. It's an emergency."

David sounded alert. "What the hell is the matter, Elliot?"

"It's George. Right lower quadrant pain, but I don't think it's appendicitis. This is the third month in a row she's had it, without telling me. I think it may be an endometrioma. I shouldn't have done it, but she was in such pain, I gave her some intravenous morphine." He finished telling David the tests he had ordered.

"I'll be there in thirty minutes," David said and hung up.

Elliot was looking at George's ultrasound films in the examining room when David hurried in.

Elliot quickly gave him a rundown of the test results and showed him the films. "You're probably right," David said, and walked to the washboard to scrub his hands. "I'll examine her and then we'll see. Relax, Elliot. She's going to be all right. You've done all the right things."

Elliot hadn't realized he was so tense, and he smiled tightly. "It scared the hell out of me."

"No wonder," David said.

They positioned her legs in the stirrups, and David quickly slipped on sterile gloves. He began his examination probing into her gently, while his other hand pressed her side.

"Well?" Elliot asked impatiently. He was standing beside the table, holding George's limp hand.

"For God's sake, Elliot, give me at least a minute!"

Suddenly both men froze. George was muttering something, her fingers weakly clutching Elliot's hand.

"Shh, sweetheart," Elliot said softly, stroking his hand over her face. "It's all right. Go back to sleep."

George felt light-headed, and so drowsy that she had to concentrate on keeping her eyes open. But it was important, she thought wildly, important to say it.

"Elliot," she whispered. "Please, it wasn't like that at all."

"I know, sweetheart," he said, soothing her.

"Please, you mustn't believe that I picked you to be the first just because of...unimportant things."

David looked sharply at Elliot, his eyes widening, but Elliot ignored him.

"I know," he said again, feeling like a dumb parrot.

"I started loving you when I served the volleyball in your stomach. I loved the way you laughed at yourself." She stared up at him, seeing him through a blurred veil. She felt his lips touch her forehead and tried to raise her face so he would kiss her. He did, very softly.

"It's all right, George," he said, lightly feathering her mouth with his lips. "I understand. Sleep now, sweetheart."

She smiled and drifted away.

George heard voices, blurred and faraway at first, then drawing closer. She blinked and slowly opened her eyes. For a moment, she had no idea where she was; then her memory cleared, and she drew in her breath, waiting for the pain. There was none. She saw Elliot and David Thornton standing at the foot of her bed, talking quietly.

"Hello," she said.

Elliot turned around quickly, the frown on his forehead instantly smoothing out.

"Hello yourself, George." He moved swiftly to her side and grasped her hand in his. "How do you feel?"

"You didn't lie to me. There is no more pain."

"There shouldn't be," David said, coming forward. "The dose Elliot gave you would make an elephant groggy." He saw that George was puzzled and quickly added, "I'll call Margaret, George. Elliot forgot she was your doctor in all the excitement."

"What's wrong with me?"

David heard the tremor in her voice. "Nothing that can't be fixed," he assured her. "Let me explain." He pulled a pen from his shirt pocket and picked up a piece of paper from her side table. "I'm much better with pictures. There's a cyst on your ovary, George." He sat beside her on the bed and proceeded to draw the female anatomy. "That's why you had the pain three months running at the same time. As the cyst got larger, the pain got worse. All we need to do is remove it, leaving your other ovary intact."

"David knows a surgeon in Los Angeles. We were just discussing when we could get him up here."

"It's not malignant or anything?" George said.

"No," Elliot said, squeezing her hand. "But the cyst could rupture, and that could be dangerous. It has to be removed well before your next period."

"It's not very major surgery, George," David said. "But delicate. That's why I want Norman Greenberg to do it. He's the best there is."

"Maggie can't do it, or you, David?"

"Norman is a perfect ten, George, in this kind of operation."

Elliot added with a grin, "Your body is far too valuable to entrust it to an imperfect nine. David and I decided to give Norman a couple more hours sleep before calling him. Likely he can be here tomorrow night and the operation on Monday morning."

George looked thoughtful. "You said, David, that the operation must be done before next month?"

"Yes."

"There's no particular rush, then?"

"George," Elliot said firmly, "let's get it done immediately. You scared the hell out of me last night. I doubt I'll sleep soundly until it's taken care of."

"I can't. I'm flying to Mexico City tomorrow, Elliot. Don't you remember?"

"To hell with Mexico City!"

George smiled. "There's something else you've forgotten," she said. "I'll be back next Friday afternoon. Then, Dr. Mallory, we're flying to Aspen for a week."

Elliot cursed softly.

"It's only two weeks, Elliot, and it is important." She saw that he would continue to argue and quickly turned to David. "How long will I be out of commission?"

"You'll be back on the volleyball court within three weeks. But you will have to rest for close to a week."

"This Norman Greenberg. Can you arrange for him to be here in two weeks, David?"

David shot a quick look at Elliot, and nodded. "When he hears who his patient is, he'd probably be here at a moment's notice."

"Can I go home now, David?"

David scratched the growth of new beard on his chin. "I'd rather you stay in the hospital today, but since you're with Elliot, I suppose it would be okay. Lord knows Elliot looks half dead. And it's already six A.M. and a Saturday. I'll call Maggie and let her know what's going on. Not to worry, all right?"

"Okay," George said. "Now, David, repeat that to Elliot!"

Chapter 10

George knew Elliot wasn't happy about her decision, but she saw no hope for it. It it were truly an emergency, she would have called Ben immediately and canceled the trip with the Braden-Tyrol people, but it wasn't. She sat up on the edge of the hospital bed, waiting for Elliot to finish her release papers, and yawned. It's like a bloody prison, she thought, and I'm on parole for two weeks.

"Hey, kid," Elliot said from the doorway in his best Humphrey Bogart voice, "you ready to split this dump?"

She turned quickly on the bed, and he saw a smile replace her somber expression. She looks like a teen-ager, he thought, with her legs dangling over the side of the bed, bare to the thighs, her hair tangled about her face.

"Yeah, big boy," she said in a ludicrous attempt at Mae West. "Ya got anything ya'd like me to wear?"

He walked around the end of the bed and came to a halt in front of her. "Only my bathrobe, George. And your panties."

"No peacock feathers?"

Teasing words formed in his mind, but he left them unspoken. He clasped her shoulders and drew her to him. "Jesus, George, you scared me."

"I scared myself," she murmured, pressing her cheek against his chest. "Thank you, Elliot."

She raised her face, and he leaned down to kiss her. "Let's go home, sweetheart."

"Okay."

"I bought you a pair of knee socks. I was saving them for a special occasion."

"Will a traumatic occasion do just as well?"

"Yes. They're lavender with pink panthers on them."

She burst into merry laughter. "Oh glory! And I thought you were tired!"

"I'd have to be dead to be that tired," he said. He unfastened the ties on the back of her gown and started to pull it off her. He looked up to see a nurse standing in the doorway.

"Yes?" he said in a far different tone of voice.

"I came to help Miss Hathaway, doctor."

He felt George start to shake. "If you laugh," he growled softly, "I'll beat you, and no knee socks. Yes, nurse, thank you. I'll be back in a few minutes, George."

"At least it's early and few people are about," the nurse said as she helped George into Elliot's bathrobe. She looked down at George's bare feet. "Well, you're going out in a wheelchair, so it won't matter."

"And here I thought hospital floors were kept spanking clean."

"Rules," the nurse said. "You're the model, aren't you?" she asked casually.

"Yes," George said, tying the belt to the bathrobe more tightly. "If anyone saw me now, I'd likely be fired."

"Oh no," the nurse said seriously. "Have you known Dr. Mallory long?"

"Her father and I are good friends," came a bland voice from the doorway. "Thank you, nurse. George, let's go."

"Is it to be the wheelchair?"

"Yes. I'll be your beast of burden." He whisked her into his arms, and set her carefully in the wheelchair.

"Oh dear," George giggled. "Are you certain someone as important as you should be pushing me. You'll cause a scandal!"

"Unfortunately," Elliot said dryly, "the night nurse in the emergency room has the biggest mouth in San Francisco. Even the janitors will know that I carried you in at three A.M. with you wearing nothing but my bathrobe."

"You're forgetting my panties, Elliot."

"Would you please be quiet?"

"Does this mean you're hopelessly compromised?"

"It means I might be arrested for child molestation," he said acidly.

"Just wait until I put on some lipstick and my new knee socks," she said.

He grinned, unable to help himself, but the events of the night soon brought a crease of worry back to his forehead.

"It will be all right, Elliot," she said calmly, easily reading his thoughts. "When we get back from Aspen, I'll submit myself to the knife."

He grunted, but said nothing.

When they arrived at Elliot's house, the knee socks weren't mentioned. They both fell into bed and slept until the afternoon.

Over dinner that evening, Elliot was abstracted.

"You are acting morose," George said severely, eyeing him over her salad.

"I want to know where you'll be staying in Mexico City. And if anything happens, George, I want you on that phone immediately."

"Yes, sir," she said, snapping him a salute.

Elliot slowly laid his fork over his plate and sat back in his chair. His long fingers formed a steeple, and he slowly drummed them together. "I want to know why you didn't tell me when you first had the pain. And no more jokes, George."

"All right, no more jokes. I thought if I ignored it, it would go away. And it did, at first."

"Why didn't you wake me up last night?

She toyed with her salad, spearing a piece of lettuce, and plucked it off her fork with her fingers. "Please don't be upset with me," she said finally. "I thought it would go away, and when it didn't it hurt too badly for me to think clearly. I'm not used to pain, and I don't think I really believed it was happening to me. What caused the cyst, Elliot?"

"No one really knows," he said. "It might possibly occur again sometime in the future."

"So I'm genetically deficient?"

"Probably too much sex in too short a period of time."

"That's dreadful!" she exclaimed, not seeing the twinkle in his eyes. "Oh, you jerk! Well, at least you're no longer morose."

He laughed and left the dining room to make them coffee. When he returned, it was George who was silent, staring down at the tablecloth.

"What is it, sweetheart?"

She raised her head, trying to think of something clever to say, but the concern in his eyes stopped her. "Will it hurt?"

"Yes, somewhat. But not nearly as much as last night. You'll feel fine after a couple of days, and then just weak and a bit sore for about a week."

She smiled at him, unwilling to let him know she was afraid. It was silly, she told herself, but she had never known a moment's illness in her life, and the thought of somebody actually cutting into her made her realize what a coward she was. Because she didn't want Elliot to worry, she said quickly, "You promised to teach me how to make coffee like yours."

"I don't know if you're up to it, George," he said gently mocking. "It requires a great deal of talent and intuition—male intuition, like all the great chefs have."

"What about Julia Child?"

He waved a dismissing hand. "An aberration."

"And Marty? You like her clam sauce."

"If you don't stop that, I'll have to concede."

"Elliot," she said, waving her fork thoughtfully at him, "you are far too intelligent to be a chauvinist. Now, if you're interested in real talent, let's watch TV. Maybe I'll be on."

Elliot groaned. "Relegated not only to TV, but to waiting for the commercials!"

George frowned, "Unfortunately, I doubt they'll be shown with sports shows. It's bound to be sitcoms."

It was. About an hour later, the commercial she had shot in England in December came onscreen. She was riding a white mare bareback, dressed in a flowing white gown, her feet bare. She rode toward a medieval castle and pulled up her horse, staring dreamily up at the crenellated ramparts. A man riding a black stallion suddenly rode out of the castle. He was as dark as she was fair, and dressed like a buccaneer, all in black. His stallion snorted at the mare, reaching out to nip her neck. The man lifted George off her horse and set her before him.

"It's a fantasy sequence," George said unnecessarily. "You would not believe how long it took Eric to get it right. The idiot barely knew the front of a horse from its rear. Now he's nuzzling my neck, most suggestive, the director thought. He had the wettest mouth, Elliot. He's English, you know."

Elliot, who had been feeling a surge of black jealousy, was forced to laugh. "As if that explains it all, huh?"

"Well," George said candidly, leaning back against him, "the only way I could look enthralled with him was to think about you."

She turned in his arms, pressing her breasts against his chest. "Well?" she asked softly.

"Well what?" he murmured, kissing her ear.

"Men," George said firmly, "are always supposed to want to make love. At least that's what I've read."

"It's true, but some men like to tease—just a bit, you understand."

She slipped her hand up beneath his sweater and began to caress him. "It's always bothered me," she said, tangling her fingers in the hair on his chest.

"What?"

"Well, women who like to make love a lot are considered, you know, promiscuous. But men can sleep with a different woman every night and it makes them more exciting. It's not fair."

"It makes them more exciting to women. Talk to your own sex, George."

"Ha! You, Dr. Mallory, thought I slept around, and it disgusted you. Admit it!"

"No, I thought you were a hooker. Vastly different. He pulled her up into his lap and nibbled her throat. "I didn't think I could afford you."

"You liar," she said poking him in the ribs. "You refuse to be serious."

"I'm through teasing," he said and lowered his mouth to hers. "I'm a simple man, George," he said between kisses. "I can only think of one thing at a time."

She felt his hands lightly caress her breasts and arched her back to offer herself more fully to him. But she was slow to respond, her mind returning again to the terrible pain and the operation. She tried to tell herself that it would be a very simple matter, but her fear of the unknown was powerful. She felt Elliot's hand on her belly, his fingers gently kneading her. She would not disappoint him, she thought fiercely, and moved sensuously against him.

"George," he said quietly, his hand now still on her stomach, "you don't have to do anything you don't want to. I don't want you fake anything with me. Do you understand?"

"I'm sorry," she said, burrowing her face against his throat.

He shook her slightly. "Don't be an ass. There's no reason for you to be sorry. You're afraid, and I don't blame you."

"Then make me forget it, if for just a little while."

"If you'll try to make me forget it, too."

"I read in a neat book once that the last perfect man lived in the twelfth century. You must be a throwback."

She felt his deep laughter and snuggled against him.

"Just wait until we have an argument," he said, pulling her to her feet. "I can be a real throwback then."

"I don't think that's going to happen any time soon," she said, and tugged him toward the bedroom.

Elliot tightened his arm about George as she slept that night, and obligingly, she moved more closely against him, her sleep unbroken. He loved her. There, he thought ruefully, he had finally admitted it to himself. What saddened him and frightened him was that she cared about him, too. She would be hurt, and there was nothing he could do about it. He thought about her perfect man and he knew himself to be very imperfect. But there was a reason to wait now. He would wait until after her operation, when she was well again, to speak to her of the future, her future. He wondered if he was rationalizing his cowardice.

Elliot sat across a table in the hospital cafeteria from Dr. Margaret Smith. He took a bite of his corned beef sandwich, grimaced and placed it carefully back onto the paper plate.

"So, Maggie," he said, "what do you think of this Norman Greenberg? Do you agree with David's choice?"

"You buy me this expensive lunch and expect to soothe my professional feelings. You know, Elliot, George prefers women doctors. She must have been very angry with you for having David come in and poke about."

"Actually, she was out of it and didn't know a thing. I think her preference for women doctors is just economic not modesty. She wants women to get rich, not men. Now, Maggie, do give me your opinion about this Greenberg fellow."

"Oh, all right," Maggie said, chewing on a french fry. "Consider my sensibilities soothed. Greenberg is just the person you want. If he leaves more than a barely visible scar, I'll be surprised. Does George want me to assist?"

"I'm sure she does."

Margaret toyed with another french fry. "When are you going to marry her, Elliot?"

"I'm not."

"I suppose from your cold tone that you don't think it's any of my business?"

Elliot smiled at her. "Right," he said. "I do wish you'd call Greenberg and go over George's history with him. I think David's already scheduled the OR."

"Yes, he has. My chairman isn't a big spender like you. He only gave me a free phone call."

"I'll chew him out if you like. He could at least have sprung for a Big Mac."

Margaret laughed and rose from the table. "David told me the delay is to let you go skiing. Don't let

George break a leg, Elliot. That would complicate things."

"George tells me she can ski rings around any miserable doctor, me included. I'll probably be the one who comes back in a cast."

"I wonder," Margaret said, eyeing him thoughtfully, "if she would stay home and nurse you? I'd supply a copy of the Kama Sutra."

"Can it, Maggie."

Chapter 11

George came through his office door looking fit, beautifully tanned and impeccably groomed in a white linen suit. She wore a light blue felt hat tilted rakishly over her forehead, and large, blue-tinted sunglasses.

"Incognito, lady?" he asked, rising to walk around his desk.

She hugged him close and laughed in his ear. "I read this book on the plane going to Mexico City that said I needed to be mysterious to keep my man."

He ignored her teasing and studied her closely. "You've felt all right?"

"Perfect, doctor, I promise."

He kissed the tip of her nose and set her away. From the corner of his eye, he saw Lisa, the picture of benevolent curiosity, standing in the doorway.

"Thank you, Lisa," he said, "for bringing Miss Hathaway in."

"Well, you know how she is, Elliot," Lisa said. "She saw your door closed, assumed, as she always does, that you were immersed in assuring the survival of the human race and wanted to bolt."

George whistled in admiration. "All that without taking a breath, Lisa! But I think I've been put down as a groupie."

"Oh no, not at all." Lisa smiled, and said to Elliot, "Shall I cancel your appointment with Dr. Howell?"

"Damn," Elliot said. "I didn't think you'd be here for another hour, George."

"No problem. I'll go home, get changed into something Aspenlike, and drink a spritzer." She nodded briskly to Elliot and Lisa, and said over her shoulder from the doorway, "I'll even dust the cobwebs off your skis. I don't want you looking like a complete duffer."

"Thanks," Elliot said dryly.

He turned back to see Lisa frowning at him. "Doesn't George know that you were state champion in Connecticut?"

"No," he said, grinning. "But she'll find out soon enough. The look on her face will be worth it!"

To Elliot's surprise, George's notion of Aspenlike clothing was not the wool pantsuit he was expecting, but a flowing black jersey dress. He cocked an eyebrow at her and said, "Is this in chapter ten of *Being Mysterious*?"

"Oh no," George said airily, whisking up her coat, "I just want to be comfortable."

"The flight is not that long, George. The skis look good. Thanks for your labor."

She laughed and followed him upstairs to his bedroom. She sat down, crossed her long, tanned legs and watched him change. He turned his back to her when he unzipped his slacks. "George," he said over his shoulder, "would you please stop staring? We're cutting the flight close as it is."

George said nothing for a moment, her eyes on the spot at the base of his spine that she loved to kiss. "I suppose now is not the time," she said.

He pulled on a pair of dark brown corduroy slacks and turned to face her. She eyed the sexy line of black hair that spread downward from his navel, and sighed. "George," he said, his voice muffled by the thick wool sweater he was jerking over his head, "prepare to be celibate. I can't imagine your mother and father wanting you sleeping with me under their parental roof."

"I hadn't thought of that," George said thoughtfully.

"Well, I have, and it's going to kill me. Come on, kid, let's get going. Believe me, this is the last flight out or I'd have booked a later one."

They made it to the boarding gate with five minutes to spare. As usual, the man assigning seats behind the counter took an unnecessarily long look at George. They were traveling first class, a treat to Elliot, since he always flew tourist. He was a bit chagrined to hear her say, "I always have seat five. Is it available?"

So much for the treat, he thought ruefully.

Once their carry-on luggage was stowed, George sat back in her seat and sighed deeply. "It's been a long day," she said, closing her eyes.

"You only called me once," Elliot said, buckling his seatbelt.

"I felt disgustingly healthy," she said. "No Montezuma's revenge, no nothing."

"You have to eat to get that."

"True. I can gain two pounds, and believe me, with my mom's cooking, I'll be dieting by day three."

The plane rose smoothly into the air, and George turned to the window to see San Francisco below them. "I never get tired of this view," she said. "I always thought I wanted to live in New York, but after being in San Francisco for two years, the thought pales."

"Would it be better for your career if you did live in New York?"

"Perhaps, at least in the future, after my contract with Braden-Tyrol runs out." She turned back and smiled at him. "We'll see."

A flight attendant came to get their drink orders. Elliot ordered a Scotch and George a ginger ale.

"I don't know why you travel first class, George. The only benefit I can see is a few more inches between seats and free drinks. And you don't even drink."

"You're right," she said quite seriously. "I never thought about it."

They had reached a cruising altitude when the flight attendant, a tall, very pretty woman, stopped at their seat.

"Excuse me," she said, a bit embarrassed. "You are the Braden-Tyrol girl, aren't you? Georgina?"

Elliot saw George's smile change just a bit to her public smile, he realized. "Yes, I am."

"Would you mind autographing these napkins for me? I promise to keep everyone else away from you."

"I'd be delighted...Marissa? What a lovely name."

"And one to Tommy and one to Candice."

Elliot leaned his head back and closed his eyes. He heard the flight attendant say in excitement, "It's such a pleasure to see you in person. I love that commercial of you in Central Park."

"Thank you. That commercial was lots of fun to make."

He heard the rustling of paper and cocked open an eye. The flight attendant was walking back down the aisle, smoothing the napkins in her hands.

"Does this happen often now?"

"Not if I wear my hat and sunglasses. But I don't mind. People are usually so nice."

George fell silent, her lovely brow furrowed in thought. Then she drew a deep breath and lightly laid her hand on Elliot's thigh.

"Dinner won't be served for another thirty minutes," she said.

"You're anxious to start gaining those two pounds?"

Her hand moved slowly up his thigh. "No. There's something else I want to do."

He looked into her eyes and said violently, "Don't be crazy George. We're in an airplane, remember?"

Her hand was caressing the inside of his upper thigh. "There's plenty of privacy in the lavatory."

He felt a surge of desire, but resolutely shook his head. "There's not enough room in the lavatory."

"It's been a week, Elliot. Aren't you just a bit interested?"

Elliot shifted in his seat. "So that's why you wore a dress," he said, shaking his head at her. "You've been planning this."

He crossed his legs, but trapped her hand between them. "It's bound to be like making love in the back seat of my father's car."

"We'll see," George said.

"Damn it, George, we'll never fit!"

She gazed at him limpidly. "We always have," she said softly.

He uncrossed his legs, only to feel her fingertips lightly touch him.

"Okay?"

He shook his head at himself. "Maybe," he said.

"Give me two minutes, then tap on the door."

He watched her walk down the aisle and disappear through the door. He looked down, thankful they were in first class, with no rows of people to notice his arousal or watch him walking after her.

He checked his watch, feeling like a complete idiot. But he was out of his seat the second the two minutes were up. He tapped lightly on the door. It opened, and he managed to squeeze inside. They were pressed together like two cards in a deck. Elliot started laughing. "George, you idiot, this is ridiculous!"

"Oh no," she said serenely. "I've thought it all out. First, you kiss me."

She wrapped her arms around his neck and pulled him down to her. Just the touch of her, the sweek scent that was peculiarly her own, made his heart race. The jersey dress outlined every curve of her, and he was content for the moment to caress her through the material.

"You are interested," she murmured into his mouth between kisses. She stood on her tiptoes, pressing herself into a better fit against him.

"What if the plane crashes?"

"What a way to go," she giggled.

He slipped his hands beneath her dress and gasped. She was naked. "Jesus," he groaned. He didn't need more of George's instructions. He lifted her onto the counter, stepped back the few inches he could, and unzipped his slacks. "George, it won't be much fun for you like this," he said.

"Yes," she said, "yes, it will."

He came into her with one thrust and lifted her against him. She wrapped her legs about his waist and buried her face against his shoulder.

He felt her strain against him, and he pushed her upward against him, his hands fiercely kneading her buttocks.

"It's been so bloody long," he groaned.

Her reply was a low moan. He felt her body stiffen, felt her legs begin to tremble around him. He whispered her name, and buried her cries in his mouth.

"Oh," she gasped, "that feels so good."

She threw her head back and arched her back, driving him deep within her. The plane hit a pocket of turbulence, and he half laughed, half moaned, as her muscles gripped him. He exploded within her.

They clung to each other, until finally Elliot managed to start to think again. "What do we do now?"

"I'm the one with the problem," she said, nibbling his ear. "You're just a disgusting male who has nothing to worry about."

"Will you be all right?" he asked softly, looking into her dazed eyes.

"I should be able to walk in another hour or so." She squeezed him. "Well, was it like making love in the back seat of your father's car?"

"I'll think about it and let you know."

He inched out of the lavatory a few moments later and ran smack into a flight attendant. He could swear he heard a muffled giggle behind him.

When George emerged, she looked as if she'd just stepped out of the pages of a fashion magazine, except for her eyes. They looked dreamy and utterly satisfied.

She sat down and snuggled against him. "We still have fifteen minutes before dinner."

"Greedy wench," he said.

She laughed and he said lightly, "I didn't have room to kiss your breasts."

Her breath hissed through her teeth. "Must you always have the last word?"

"The last thrust, in any case."

The flight attendant who served their dinner was the same one who had passed him in the aisle.

"I'm sure you must be hungry," she said blandly, setting his tray down in front of him.

"Why do you think I ordered the rare beef?" Elliot returned, just as blandly.

The flight attendant nodded. "You're right, of course. Flying is an exhausting business. It's wise to keep your strength up."

Elliot censored several crude retorts, and said, "A lot of things need to be kept up...even the plane."

"So true," the flight attendant agreed, an unholy twinkle in her eyes.

"What was that all about?" George demanded once they were alone again.

"Just a little tit for tat. She knew exactly what we were doing, George."

"I think she tatted you pretty well."

"Well, I didn't have a chance to ti—"

"Don't you dare say it, Elliot Mallory! Eat your dinner and think elevating thoughts."

"A bad pun, George, very bad."

George was the one who became quiet. She only picked at her dinner.

"You're feeling all right, aren't you?" Elliot asked finally.

"Of course." She eyed him a moment, her expression anxious. "Elliot, I want to talk to you. In a minute," she added, seeing the flight attendant return to take their trays.

Elliot waited patiently, imagining that she wanted to talk about the operation.

He was utterly taken aback when she turned in her seat, and blurted out, "Will you marry me?"

He was taken utterly off guard and could only stare at her. Her eyes were shining with excitement. He felt a fist squeeze at his heart, his breath catching in his throat. That she would take the initiative had never occurred to him. Another example, he thought frantically, of the difference in their ages. A woman his age would never do such a thing. He didn't know what to say. He tore his gaze from hers, the *no* and the reasons for it trembling on his lips. He remembered her operation. He had to be certain she would go through with it. Very slowly, to gain time, he repeated, "Marry you?"

"I didn't mean to shock you," she said, squeezing his arm. "I want to marry you very much, Elliot. I love you, and I want to spend my life with you. We're compatible. We don't fight much. I very much enjoy sex with you."

"George," he said, raising his hand to stem the tide.

"Elliot, I know I'm young, but not that young. And I wouldn't be a parasite or a drain on you. My income is increasing steadily, with a big leap this year. I own two apartment houses in the Upper Haight, me and the bank, that is. I could give you the name of my accountant and she could give you a complete rundown of all my assets. My money isn't particularly liquid, but —"

"George, for God's sake, I don't give a damn about your money!"

She nodded eagerly. "No, I'm sure that you don't care any more about my money than I do about yours. But I wanted you to know that I would pull my weight. Elliot, it's not just sex. You're a wonderful cook, and you make me laugh, and we have such fun together." He didn't reply, and she plunged onward, "If you want, I could take some more college courses. I know you probably think I'm appallingly ignorant. I don't want you to ever be ashamed of me."

"George, you are not ignorant. If you ever wanted to go back to school, you would do it for yourself, not me. As to my being ashamed of you, don't be a turkey."

She smiled happily. "Then you do love me? You will marry me?"

He closed his eyes a moment, swallowing all the arguments he had prepared to give her when she was well again after the operation. He turned in his seat to face her. "George," he said quietly, "you've taken me by surprise." That was certainly the truth! "I haven't thought of marriage. It's a very big step, a big decision." That was a bloody lie, and he was sounding evasive, like a woman who had just received a marriage proposal she found inconvenient. "Give me time to think about it. All right?"

She searched his face anxiously.

"And you think more about it." *You're twenty-three and I'm thirty-eight! You have everything ahead of you.*

"I have," she said. She dropped her eyes to her hands, clasped together in her lap. "I suppose I did take you off guard. I don't mean to rush you, Elliot."

"I know," he said, swallowing. He repeated steadily, "Give me some time, George."

"I forgot to tell you that I would be happy to handle your investments for you, if you wish."

Shakespeare was right, Elliot thought, a smile tugging at his mouth. There's nothing like the comic to temper the tragic.

"I might consider that, George," he said, a laugh breaking through the knot of misery in his throat.

Chapter 12

Didn't I promise you bedlam?" George whispered in Elliot's ear.

"Utter bedlam and delight," he said, helping her into her chair at the dining-room table.

The five children George had promised, all under the age of seven, were so full of exuberant energy and excitement that Elliot wondered if he could trade in his glass of wine for a stiff Scotch, neat. The dinner table was loaded with enough food for a battalion, to Elliot's eye, but George assured him it was just an ordinary meal when the family was all together.

Tammy, Derek's wife, was busily serving up plates for their three children. She was a tall woman, dark-haired, a bit on the plump side and utterly impervious to her children's noise. Derek, George's oldest brother, was a large, athletic man of about thirty-five who seemed to have George's outgoing personality, with quite a bit of devilry thrown in. He raised his voice over the racket as he shoved a plate of fried chicken and potato salad in front of his three-year-old. "Don't expire, Elliot! You'll get used to it, that or you'll be out on the slopes twenty-four hours a day to escape."

Elliot smiled and replied during a brief lull, "George tells me you're a businessman. What do you do?"

Jason Hathaway, the middle brother, a slender, rather stoop-shouldered young man with George's near-violet eyes, hooted with laughter. "Would you believe toilets?"

His wife, Irene, poked him in the side. "Come on, jerk! Don't believe him, Elliot; Derek is a designer and consultant for very futuristic bathrooms and kitchens.

"We call him Johnny Come Lately; J.C.L. for short," Tod called out.

Duke Hathaway raised a quieting hand, and to Elliot's surprise, even the children grew instantly still. "Before you know more than you want about the Hathaway family, Elliot, let me say that we're delighted you came." He gave George a lazy smile and raised his wineglass. "Here's to a week of great skiing with no broken bones!"

"Well, we've got a doctor here to take care of us," Tod said. "I've always said George is a smart cookie, always plans ahead."

"At least he's worth more than a pitcher who can't strike out a little league," George said.

"You mean he won't tell us to take two aspirin and send him fifty dollars?" Derek asked.

"He'd tell you to take a dose of arsenic and jump off the ski lift, big brother," George retorted. "As for you, Tod the Dodge, he'd advise you to get a new pitching arm before the season starts.''

"George needs to come down a peg," Tod said. "All this fame is going to her head and mouth."

"Now, now, brother," Jason said. "The only reason anyone watches you play baseball on TV is because of the commercials."

Mrs. Hathaway, who was smiling calmly at the flying jabs that followed, turned to Elliot. "It's so nice to have the family together. I hope the children never change."

"George tells me you come here every year to ski?"

"Yes. We bought the cabin some ten years ago."

"I don't think I'd call it a mere cabin," Elliot said, staring around the large dining room.

"Well, no, I suppose not. We have Duke to thank for that, else we'd be piled up like rugs in a department store. He always told me that we'd better plan ahead for grandchildren. The five bedrooms are already full, and Tod and George aren't even married yet. Do you come from a large family, Elliot?"

"Just one sister, Lindy, and two nephews and a niece. I have a feeling this is going to be quite an educational week."

"Oh, this is nothing. Wait until they really get going. Would you like some baked beans?"

Elliot shook his head. "George looks quite a bit like you, Mrs. Hathaway."

"Dorothy, please. Thank you for saying so. I've always thought the raw materials were lurking about in me and came together in George. Her height and figure come from her grandmother. As for that financial intuition she has, none of us can figure that out."

"She's been badgering me to let her take over my investments, what there are of them."

"I'd let her," Dorothy said. "She's been advising her father and me for three years now. Her brother Derek hooted with male disdain when he heard about it, but Tammy told me that during the past year, Derek would come up with an idea, chew it over for a couple of days and then get on the phone to his sister. Tammy, of course, thinks it's marvelous. She's a nurse and champing at the bit to get back to her profession. You'll hear some real heady arguments when George and Derek get going about women leaving-their-babies-in-the-hands-of-strangers. I believe you've already met Tod?"

Elliot nodded, glancing toward the handsome youngest brother, who was lounging back in his chair flying a chicken wing toward one of his nieces.

"George dragged you to one of the A's games?"

"Yes, but she neglected to tell me that the pitcher was her brother."

Dorothy Hathaway laughed. "You're not a baseball fan then?"

"Let's say I'm becoming accustomed. Actually, until now, I haven't watched much baseball."

"Well, all my kids seem to have been interested in most sports."

"Except swimming?" Elliot asked.

"That's true, although George told me some months ago that she was taking it up. As for Jason, he was an excellent golfer until he became infatuated with computers. I'm afraid his nine irons are rusting in the closet. This year I doubt he'll have a prayer armwrestling with any of his brothers. But he is a good skier."

"Jason is a programmer?"

"That too. He owns his own company now."

Elliot laughed. "It appears I'm surrounded by ov- erachievers."

"Yes, isn't it marvelous?" Dorothy said compla- cently. "I've never been able to figure it out. Here I am, a dirt farmer's daughter."

"I bet there was oil under that dirt!"

"I suppose I should give some credit to Duke. Tod, get that bone out of Ginger's ear!"

Elliot waited until Ginger's ear was back in place, then said quietly to Dorothy Hathaway, "Perhaps there's a question you can answer for me." He paused a moment, fiddling with his potato salad. "George is beautiful, in fact her looks are quite spectacular. But she has no conceit that I've ever seen. Whenever I or anyone else comment on her looks, she just tosses it off, says it's a good thing or else she wouldn't have a job."

"And you can't understand it?"

"Frankly, no. I keep waiting for a little conceit, or a little pleased recognition of her looks, to surface."

"Her grandmother's influence, I think. You see, her grandmother, Camilla, my mother, was beautiful. She died beautiful a couple of years ago at nearly eighty. Good bone structure and all that. In any case, Cam- illa kept an eagle eye on George while she was grow- ing up. If George ever showed any signs of conceit, she promptly took her down a peg or two. And, of course, there are her brothers. They're more interested in her jockdom than in her beauty. They don't really look at her like you do or like strangers do. Does that make any sense?"

"I suppose it does. I would like to have met her grandmother."

"She was a grand old lady. We all miss her." Dorothy turned to pour some milk into a grandchild's glass.

George took the opportunity to whisper to Elliot, "Did Mother tell you how great we all are?"

"Paragons, the lot of you. I listened politely."

"I'll bet your mother is the same way. Can't wait to crow about her brilliant son."

"At least it's all true," he said blandly.

"I think that bone that was in Ginger's ear belongs in your mouth."

"Now, George, if you can't compete, don't play the game."

"Dr. Mallory," Tammy Hathaway called over the table, "you're the chairman of the Radiology Department?"

"Yes, and call me Elliot. I understand you're a nurse."

Tammy shot a sideways glance at her husband. "Yes, and next year I'm going back."

"Now, Tammy," Derek said, his brows lowering. "The children need—"

George burst into merry laughter. "We've only been together for two hours and you've already got my blood boiling, Derek!"

"A truce," Duke Hathaway said, "at least for the duration of dinner."

"Yeah, Der," Jason called. "Go design a new john, Johnny!"

"Wait until I get my hands on you, circuit brain!"

"I'm going to flush both of you down," Tod called out.

"And on and on," George said.

"I don't think anyone could ever die of boredom in your family, George," Elliot said.

"No, but burst blood vessels are another matter. What do you think of Mariana? It's odd," she added, frowning thoughtfully. "She's the first woman Tod hasn't had me check out."

Mariana Hammond was very beautiful and very quiet. She appeared rather dazed by all the noise, but Elliot thought he saw a smile lurking in her brown eyes.

"Maybe playboy Tod is serious," Elliot said.

"Hmmm," George said. "Well, everyone started checking you out the minute you walked through the door. Mariana," she called out, "where did you meet my clod of a brother?"

The deep brown eyes lowered a moment. "At a charity ball. Tod was our guest of honor."

"Ah, jock of the night, huh?"

"George," Tod mocked, "never just one night!"

"You've been had again, sweetheart," Elliot said under the cover of laughter that erupted around the table. To his delight, George was actually blushing.

Suddenly, there were several gasps. Mariana Hammond had leaned over in her chair and dumped the rest of her wine down Tod's shirt.

He yelped, leaped up in his chair and collapsed again as his nieces and nephews and siblings went into gales of laughter.

"Good for you, Mariana," Mr. Hathaway said. "Would you like some more wine?"

"Dad, whose side are you on?" Tod complained, wiping off his shirt with a napkin.

"My dear Tod," Mr. Hathaway said gently, "look at your mother and your sister. Need you ask?"

"I would love some more wine, sir," Mariana said calmly.

Elliot had imagined that after-dinner coffee in the living room would be conducted in a more subdued way. He was wrong. The children were packed off to bed, but despite the huge meal, the four Hathaway siblings were still in tearing spirits. Elliot sat down next to Mariana Hammond, watching their antics from the corner of his eye.

"I understand you arrived last evening?"

"Yes. I had my introductions over a dinner of four gallons of Irish stew."

"You, I take it, aren't from a large family."

"No, I'm an only child."

"You live in San Francisco, Mariana?"

"In Mill Valley," she said, smiling toward Jason and George, who were on their stomachs on the floor, arm wrestling.

"What do you do with your time?"

She shrugged, elegantly. "Nothing, really."

"Oh," Elliot said, rather daunted.

There was a shout of laughter as Jason dragged George's arm down to the carpet.

Elliot sipped at his coffee.

"George looks quite different in person."

Oh no, Elliot thought. Now for some cattiness.

"If anything," Mariana continued thoughtfully, "she's even more beautiful. One wonders how that can be true with her in jeans and a western shirt and look at those socks—lavender with pink panthers—but it is."

Elliot decided that Mariana Hammond, whatever else she was, was a very honest person.

"George has a fondness for unusual knee socks," he said.

"Derek, you ape! Put me down!"

Elliot looked up to see Derek swinging George above his head.

"If you were my equal, George, you wouldn't be such a weakling. My God, circuit brain beat you at arm wrestling! Hey, Elliot, do you want her?"

Elliot quickly set down his coffee cup and jumped to his feet, just in time to catch George. He grinned to himself, stumbled backward, groaning loudly, and fell to the floor with George on top of him.

There was an awful moment of silence.

George scrambled off him. "Elliot!" She grabbed his hand and felt for his pulse. "You idiot!" she shouted at her brother. "He's hurt!"

Elliot couldn't help himself. He started laughing. He looked up at George's stricken face and watched her expression change from disbelief to red-faced chagrin. He clutched his stomach with laughter, and rolled onto his side.

"You jerk!" George yelled at him. "You scared the wits out of me!" She started pummeling him with her fists. Elliot grabbed her wrists and pulled her down beside him.

"Now," he said softly, "you have an idea of how I felt."

She stopped struggling, but she was still frowning. "That wasn't fair."

"You don't think we're even now?"

She pursed her lips. "No," she said, "I don't think we are."

Elliot shot her a look of mock terror. "Lord, what am I in for now, I wonder?"

Duke Hathaway called a halt at midnight. "We'll have great skiing tomorrow. All of you off to bed. Breakfast is at seven o'clock."

"Your famous blueberry pancakes, Dad?" George asked.

"You got it, cookie. And lots of sausage for my growing boys."

"I think Derek should have half a grapefruit," George said. "He has an inch to pinch; I checked him out."

"Just because I can play 'Oh, Susanna' on your ribs, George..."

Elliot left George at her bedroom door. "I think," she said softly, "that Tod and Mariana are still downstairs necking. Wanna come in for a nightcap, sailor?"

He rubbed his knuckles along her jaw and smoothed her hair behind her ear. "Under their roof, George, we'll exercise restraint." He pulled her gently against him and kissed her lightly. "Good night, sweetheart. Sleep well."

"Drat," George grumbled. "I will sleep, but I don't know how well."

The sun was brilliant against the snow, and the air was crystal clean. Snow-dusted pine trees lined the trail. George was skiing in front of Elliot, wearing a red ski outfit that outlined every perfect pound of her, a red wool cap and goggles. Her form was smooth, her movements lithe and supple. She turned her head and waved at him, then executed a full turn in the air as she flew off a mogul.

"Kid stuff, George," he called after her. He heard her clear laughter and easily copied her turn.

George reached the bottom of the run and came to a stop, turning to watch him.

"I must say, cowboy, you're not exactly a beginner," she said, eyeing him judiciously.

"You're the only one who assumed I was, George," he said.

"You also look good enough to eat." Her eyes wandered over his teal-blue ski outfit.

"Wait until you see my green. A perfect match for my eyes."

"Conceited jerk!" she said amiably. "You ready for a rest? I saw Mom and Dad head into the lodge on the last run."

They unfastened their skis and leaned them and their poles against the stone wall of the lodge.

"We were really lucky," George said, pulling off her goggles and cap. "When Mom and Dad bought the cabin, the lodge hadn't been built yet. The developer who bought the land wanted to buy them out, but they refused. So we're only a ten-minute hike from the center of the course. The only drawback is all the tourists."

"It has spread out quite a bit. It's been several years since I've skied here," Elliot said.

"Have you ever raced?"

"Yes," Elliot said, "a bit. Would you care to get creamed this afternoon?"

"Your confidence is exceeded by little else."

He was laughing when they joined George's parents. "Where are the kids?"

"We take shifts," Dorothy said. "Since this is your first visit, Elliot, you won't have to watch three children on the beginners' slope."

"I don't mind," Elliot said politely, accepting a hot cup of coffee from a waiter.

George shot him an incredulous look before moving to the huge stone fireplace and warming her hands. The lobby of the lodge was filling rapidly, and Elliot joined her, leaving her parents with the only two available chairs.

"The old West was never like this," George said, "although I appreciate their efforts."

Elliot eyed the eighteen-foot-high beamed ceilings, the rough oak Western furniture, and the hooked rugs that covered the wood floors. "It beats the No-Tell Motel."

"For sure, for sure," George said in her best Valley Girl imitation. She lowered her eyes a moment to her cup of hot chocolate. "Have you thought about... well, what I asked you on the plane?"

"You mean there's a private lavatory around?"

Her cheeks, already rosy with color, flushed deeper, and there was a wary look in her eyes.

"Yes, George," he said quietly. "But—"

"But what?"

He sighed, avoiding her eyes. "Time, George." He wanted to shout at her that he was too old to be her oldest brother, let alone her husband.

George regarded him silently for a moment, then smiled up at him, a dazzlingly brilliant smile that made him want to fling her to the floor and love her until she was breathless.

"After lunch, do you really want to give the kids a shot on the beginners's slope?"

"Absolutely," he said. "Tomorrow, I'll teach you how to race downhill."

To Elliot's surprise, the three young Hathaways were eager to do anything he told them to. And they were good. "Children," he said to George, shaking his head. "They know no fear."

"None at all. Derek, Jr. broke his leg last year and it didn't faze him."

"Look at Kathy," he said, pointing to Jason's daughter. "Bend your knees," he called to her. "That's it, now snowplow!"

"Yes," George said slowly, staring at her niece, "I'm looking." And she was thinking, for the first time, of having Elliot's children. For a perfect moment, she pictured them on skis, laughing, waving plump little hands, tumbling with their parents in the snow....

"Are you in never-never land, George?"

"What? Oh, no, I was just thinking."

"About my condos in Santa Barbara?"

Keep it light, George, she thought. "Exactly," she said. "And I do have some suggestions about that, Elliot."

"And here I was telling Maggie that you wanted only women to get rich."

"Oh, Dr. Smith. When did you see her?"

"Early last week, to apologize for calling David and not her. She wondered if you were embarrassed with David poking around, and I told her it was a matter of money and success for women and had nothing to do with modesty."

"Did David...poke around?"

"Not much," he lied smoothly.

"I don't believe you, and I'll never be able to face him again," George said firmly.

"Well," he said, unable to help himself, "he really wasn't all that concerned with your face."

She caught him off guard and he landed on his back in a snowbank. "I'll get you for that, Elliot Mallory! Just you wait!"

He came up balancing on his elbows and laughed at her. "What will you do, George? Call a woman doctor for me?"

He ducked a snowball. Within minutes, the three children had shed their skis and were flinging snowballs with them as fast as they could pack them.

Chapter 13

On Wednesday, over a dinner of six large pizzas, Duke Hathaway proclaimed Elliot King of the Slopes. He had won the downhill race handily, George his closest competition. Jason was given the Face in the Snow award and crowned with a hastily strung circle of pepperonis.

"Pretty good for a lazy doctor," George teased him.

"It's all the swimming," Elliot said, saluting her with a beer. "You might have a chance against me if you could manage to swim more than six laps."

He was smiling at her, feeling very relaxed, until Dorothy said to him, "You fit right in, Elliot. I don't think George could ever really be happy with someone who wasn't as athletic as she."

He nearly choked on his beer. It had been easy, too easy, to become one of them, to laugh and horse around with them, to begin to hug George in their presence. Duke Hathaway had even seen him kissing his daughter rather passionately outside her bedroom door. But surely they couldn't want George to marry a man old enough to be her father. Not quite that old, he amended to himself, gazing toward the silver-haired Duke, but still...As if in answer to his thoughts, Dorothy continued serenely, "George has always been older than boys her own age. I suppose it comes from being so much with her brothers. That and the fact that George always intimidated the young men who wanted to date her."

"She is very beautiful," Elliot said cautiously.

"Oh, it's not that, I don't think," Dorothy said. "I know that I wasn't at all like George when I was eighteen, or twenty-three, for that matter. She's very mature."

Elliot carefully set down his beer mug. "I am sure," he said to Dorothy, his voice clear and low, "that George can find a young man who will not be intimidated by her."

After a brief pause, Dorothy said lightly, "You're likely right. The week has gone by so quickly. I hate to think that Friday we'll be spread all over the country again."

It reminded him that George would have her operation on Monday. She had insisted that her family not be told. When he asked her why, she had said with a crooked smile, "You can't imagine what kind of grief I would have to put up with all week! A Woman's Problem—can't you just hear Derek?"

Dorothy thought her remaining slice of pizza tasted like congealed cheese. She wasn't blind. George's happiness was like a beacon, and she knew without a second thought that her daughter was sleeping with Elliot. There was a new softness about her, an unspoken intimacy that existed between them. She had assumed that George would marry him. He was, after all, the first man she had ever brought to meet the family. It simply hadn't occurred to her that Elliot might not be equally head over heels in love with her daughter. But he was, she thought, frowning slightly. One had but to look at him looking at George. She didn't understand it. She heard her daughter's delighted laughter at something Derek said, and felt tears sting her eyes.

After dinner, George grabbed Elliot's hand. "Let's go for a walk. It's stopped snowing."

"Where do you get all this energy?" he asked her.

"Well, I'm not using it on...other things," she confided.

The night was cold and clear, the newly fallen snow crunchy beneath their boots.

"This has been the best year of all," George said.

He grunted in reply.

"I hope you like my family?"

"Better than a circus." He paused a moment, knowing she wanted to hear more. "Your parents are very caring people."

"Do you like everyone?"

"Only Scrooge could dislike any of them."

She was silent for a moment, then accused him, "You've raced competitively before, haven't you?"

He laughed at her, relieved. "Well, I was state champion in Connecticut some fifteen years ago. When you were eight years old, George," he added.

"Did you ever think about the Olympics?"

"Good God no! Even if you think I'm the greatest jock in the world, George, I'm still a duffer compared to people of Olympic caliber."

"I suppose you're right," she conceded unwillingly. She came to a stop on the rise that overlooked the lodge. "It's so beautiful, all the lights, and you can't hear a single tourist from here." She turned to face him and looked intently up at him. "You've been awfully quiet since dinner. Did you expect a crown of pepperonis with your award?"

"Indeed, and I was gravely disappointed."

Suddenly, George thought she didn't know him at all. He was charming, as always, but he was evading her. She remembered thinking months ago that he was out of her league. She thought so again. She forced a smile to her lips. It was too dark for him to see that it didn't reach her eyes.

"I'm cold. Even my black knee socks aren't enough."

She tucked her arm through his, and they tromped back through the snow to the cabin.

Elliot was standing next to Derek and Tammy and Mr. and Mrs. Hathaway in front of the lodge the following afternoon, waiting for George to finish her run. His eyes lit up when she came into view in a flash of powder blue.

"That's my girl," Duke said.

She looked up and waved one of her poles. Suddenly, she appeared to lose her balance and clipped a mogul. Elliot watched, horrified, as her poles went flying and she twisted in the air and came down in a tuck position, her skis slipping loose of her binders. She slid in the snow for several feet, rolling over onto her back, and lay utterly still.

"Oh, my God," Elliot gasped. He raced toward her, his gut wrenching in fear.

He heard Duke Hathaway calling him, but didn't slow until he reached George. She was sprawled on her back, her arms and legs spread in the snow. He dropped to his knees beside her. He drew a quick breath and forced himself to do a methodical examination. The pulse in her throat was strong. He stared down at her still face for a moment, afraid to touch her. Get a hold of yourself, he told himself sternly. Gently, he lifted her eyelids. There was a flutter of movement.

"George," he said, lightly slapping her cheeks. "Come on, sweetheart."

To his utter confusion, she opened her eyes and winked at him. In the next moment, she came up swiftly on her knees and tossed a hastily packed snowball in his face.

"Gotcha," she said with great satisfaction.

He sat back on his heels, aware now of the laughter coming from behind him. "That was all an act?" he asked slowly.

"Been doing it for years," she said. "I usually do a full twist in the air, but I was going too slow to give you my Class-A performance."

His surge of relief was quickly replaced by a blast of anger.

"My revenge," she said, unaware that he was not amused. "Now, doctor, we're even!"

"Damn you!" he growled at her. He jumped to his feet, grabbed her arm and jerked her upright. "Don't you ever do anything like that again! You damned little idiot—" He broke off, swore crudely and pulled her after him.

"My skis, Elliot!"

"To hell with your skis!"

Derek looked on with growing amusement. "I think," he said to his wife and parents, "that George has finally met her match."

"George up to her tricks?" Jason asked, trudging over to the group.

"Yep." Derek shrugged, watching Elliot drag his sister up the slope toward the cabin.

"I don't think," Duke said slowly, "that any of us should return to the cabin for a while."

"Elliot," George yelped, trying to pull away from him, "let me go. Good lord, my family's watching!"

"Let them," he said grimly. "They're likely applauding."

He opened the cabin door and pulled her inside. No one else was about.

"Now what are you going to do?" George demanded. "It was just a joke, Elliot."

"I'm going to beat the hell out of you," he said even more grimly.

She turned and fled up the stairs, Elliot at her heels.

He grabbed her midway up and flung her over his shoulder. "Good grief, you idiot, put me down!"

"Not on your life, lady!" He kicked open the door to his bedroom, slammed it shut with his shoulder and tossed George on the bed. "You scared me to death," he said in a very low voice, then grabbed her around the waist and pulled her over his thighs. His hand came down hard on her buttocks. He smacked her several more times, then flung her off him onto her back on the bed. She lay there, staring at him.

"Well," he snapped. "What do you have to say now?"

To his consternation, a large tear welled up and trickled down her cheek. He cursed softly, grabbed her and pulled her into his arms.

He felt no resistance in her and slowly gentled his kiss. He tasted the salty tears on her mouth. He was trembling, from the shock of his anger and now from desire. His hands went wild at her clothes. George vaguely understood what was happening to him, and she lay passively as he stripped her. Her heart was pounding, and her bottom didn't hurt at all.

Elliot stood up and quickly pulled off his clothes. He came down on top of her naked, pinning her arms above her head, and he kissed her, all his anger turned to passion.

"Elliot," she whispered into his mouth. He let her arms go and she clutched him to her. When he finally entered her, she was eager for him, her senses heightened by the days of sexual tension between them. Their mating was brief and violent. Elliot collapsed over her, his breathing hoarse in her ears.

"I'm sorry," she whispered. "Please don't be angry with me."

"Did I hurt you?" he asked, raising himself over her on his elbows. He looked intently into her eyes.

"My bottom," she said.

"That you deserved." He was silent a moment, his gaze shifting from her eyes. "I didn't even think about your pleasure. I'm sorry."

"If you had, I'd likely be dead."

He smiled at her, reluctantly, and rolled to his back, holding her against him. He felt exhausted, and disgusted at himself for his loss of control. The chill air touched him, and he pulled a thick quilt over them.

"That was a performance worthy of a macho romatic hero," she said with some satisfaction as she settled herself against his side.

He turned on his side, facing her, his expression startled. "Romantic hero?" he said blankly.

"Oh yes," she said, nibbling at his chin. "A romantic hero is always carried away by passion. He's unable to help himself, you see."

"I don't see anything romantic about it," he said dryly.

"It's a marvelous fantasy. What's supposed to happen is that the man is a terrible womanizer, changes women as often as his socks, until he meets the Right Woman. He treats her badly, of course, until he realizes toward the end that he can't live without her. Then he turns magically into a sweet, lovable, probably thoroughly boring person."

"You're putting me on," he said roughly.

"Never," she said positively. "Don't you see—in the romantic-hero fantasy, the man is all sorts of experienced, very worldly, but he has to forget all of that and become utterly faithful, and of course very gentle and tender with the heroine."

"Do you have that fantasy, George?" he asked her.

Her eyes crinkled in laughter. "Why, of course, doctor. Weren't you just marvelously violent and nasty to me?"

"Hell," he said. "George, are you laughing at me?" You little—"

"I'm sorry, Elliot. Please don't tickle me. I'm too weak from all your exertions."

"I am too." He sighed. "I much prefer being lovable and thoroughly boring all the time."

"Never that," she said sleepily. "Never that."

He kissed the back of her neck, smoothing away her long hair. "Do you know that you have little sexy female curls on the nape of your neck?"

"Little sexy curls? Oh mercy!"

"Don't forget female."

Elliot hugged her more closely to him, and closed his eyes. In the next moment, he was asleep.

George felt sore, confused and happy. He cared about her, she thought drowsily, else he wouldn't have been so angry with her. It didn't occur to her that the house would soon be filled with people. She snuggled closer to him and fell asleep.

"Oh my God!"

George raised her head, blinking away sleep.

"It's dark!" Elliot looked frantically at the clock on the bedside table. Eight-thirty. He felt utterly mortified. He had made love to her without a thought to her family and proceeded to compound his idiocy by falling asleep like a damned fool.

"I'm sure Mom has left us some dinner," George said.

He cursed.

George giggled. "I think everyone will know what we've been doing."

He cursed again.

"Elliot," she said reasonably, "we're not teenagers. And you did cart me off in front of my parents like a caveman. If they had been the least bit concerned, they would have come to rescue me."

"They probably should have," he said. He sighed, turned on the lamp beside the bed and gazed about at their scattered clothing. "Nothing for it, I guess, but to face the music."

The first strain of music was from five-year-old Derek, Jr. "Aunt George, you slept through dinner! We had chicken again. It was baked this time."

"I think your Aunt George is in need of a steak," Tod observed blandly. "Elliot too. Rare."

"Tod," Mariana said, her eyes narrowing.

"Chicken will be just fine," George said.

"It's all in the oven, dear," Dorothy said.

Elliot had hoped they would eat their belated dinner in private. He soon discovered what a forlorn hope it was. All the brothers and their women gathered at the table.

"The children are in bed," Jason said to no one in particular.

George arched a brow at him, "What does that mean? You can be outrageous?"

"Well," Tod drawled, "you'll notice that Mom and Dad aren't here either."

George groaned and waved a chicken bone in Tod's face. "I'll thank you, Tod, not to embarrass Elliot."

"Elliot?" Derek said. "He's a man, kiddo. It's you, my little virgin sister, who should be embarrassed."

Tammy poked her husband in the ribs. "Cut it out, Der. George is not a child. Lord knows your accountant doesn't think so!"

George suddenly realized that Tod was still wearing his ski outfit. She wondered if he had come into the bedroom he was sharing with Elliot. At least he hadn't stayed to change his clothes. She blushed.

"Ah, George," Tod said, his eyes twinkling wickedly, "I do wonder what you are thinking."

"You probably wouldn't understand," Mariana said. "You are the most insensitive clod I've ever met."

"Not clod," George said. "Dumb jock."

"It comes to the same thing," Mariana said. "If it weren't for his family, I would have thrown him over ages ago."

Elliot drew a brief, relieved sigh. At least the cannon fire was aimed at someone else now. He wondered if he should say anything. Say what, you fool? he thought, laughing at himself.

"Mariana," Tod said, "if you don't control your mouth I won't marry you."

"You, marry?" George gasped.

"The Playboy of the Bay Area? I don't believe it!" Derek said.

Tammy eyed her brother-in-law thoughtfully. "Mariana is much too smart to hook up with you, Tod. I suggest you try for a bit of humility if you cherish any hopes in that direction."

Mariana was smiling crookedly, her fingers on Tod's sleeve. "I'll never forget his come-on line," she said to the group at large. "He invited me to his apartment, not to see his etchings, mind you, but to see photos of his fastball."

"That's probably the only area where he has any control at all," Derek said over the laughter.

"I think," Tod muttered, "that's enough."

"Poor baby," George mocked him. "Are we besmirching your reputation?"

"Give him a dictionary, George!" Jason hooted.

"All right, circuit brain," Tod threatened. "You might still be able to beat up George, but I—"

"Tod," George said to Elliot, "always uses threats of brawn when a little wit would carry him through."

"At least my clothes weren't strewed all over the bedroom floor!" Tod roared.

Mariana reached over and patted Tod's arm. "Now, now," she said sweetly, "you mustn't show your jealousy quite so blatantly."

"Well," Tod grumbled, a reluctant smile turning up the corners of his mouth, "I am getting tired of necking on that damned sofa."

There was a throat-clearing hum from the doorway. "Excuse me, children," Dorothy Hathaway said. "Keep it down or you'll wake the little children."

"Hey, Mom," Derek said, "will we still be children when we're sixty?"

"Some of you will be, undoubtedly," Dorothy said. She shook her head a moment, a faraway smile lighting her eyes. "I suppose you're all over twenty-one now. And that *damned* sofa was the favorite piece of furniture for all the boys in the cabin. Tammy, do you remember when Derek wrenched his back on the sofa from all his...exertions?"

"Oh, I remember all right. The baby! I've had to kiss it and make it well for thirteen years now."

"At least I let you make an honest man of me!" Derek said. He rose from his chair and smiled wickedly at George and Elliot. "Since Tammy and I are legal, unlike you, I think I'll cart her off now. Eat your hearts out, guys!"

Some fifteen minutes later, Elliot found himself alone with Jason Hathaway, George having dashed upstairs to have her turn in the shower.

"The first time George pulled that stunt," Jason said, fiddling with his coffee cup, "Mom and Dad nearly had a cardiac arrest. She was nine years old."

Elliot smiled ruefully. "She scared the hell out of me."

"One of us should have warned you, I guess." He grinned. "You should have seen the look on your face."

"No thanks," Elliot said dryly.

Jason was silent a moment, then said slowly, "As you know, Irene and I live near Philadelphia. When George turned up on TV, you wouldn't believe the razzing I got from people at work. A couple of guys took turns showing up at my office door on their hands and knees, panting and begging for her address. I have to admit I've wondered how you handle it."

"In what way?" Elliot asked, quirking a dark brow.

"Like when she's asked for her autograph. Has that happened yet?"

"Yes, it has. I see what you mean now. It was a bit disconcerting the first couple of times, but now—" He shrugged his shoulders.

"No," Jason said thoughtfully, "I didn't think you'd be intimidated. You know, being the escort for my gorgeous sister."

"Tattered ego? No, I don't think so. George makes so little of it, you see."

Jason smiled and rose. "I didn't mean to pry," he said. "I'm going to watch some TV. Want to join me?"

"All right." Elliot grinned. "Maybe we'll see George kissing a bottle of perfume."

Chapter 14

I've got a surprise for you, Elliot."

Elliot turned in his plane seat and smiled whimsically at George. "Not again?"

"Oh no," she assured him. "I figure if you get a perfect ten at thirty-five-thousand feet, there's only one direction to go. Now, I'll give you twenty guesses, but you'll never get it."

"You bought me a gift certificate to the Mustang Ranch."

"Elliot!"

He stoked his fingertip over her jaw. "Blushing, George? It is a legal brothel, you know." He sighed deeply. "I guess that's not it, huh?"

"No, you lecher!"

"Well, since we get free booze in first class, let me swill a while to invigorate my brain."

Elliot exhausted his twentieth guess by the time the plane was nearing the San Francisco airport. "All right. I give up. I've fastened my seatbelt. Lay it on me."

"Tomorrow morning, my dear, you and I are going to get out of bed at 4:30 A.M."

"You're crazy."

"No, no, seriously! And I'm going to make a phone call," she added in a mysterious voice.

"To whom? My mother?"

"No, to Napa. And if the weather is okay, you and I are then going to drive to Napa and at 6:00 A.M. we're going to pile into a hot-air balloon."

His eyes lit up. "How did you know I wanted to do that? I swear I've never said anything about it to you. Great surprise, George!" He leaned over and gave her a smacking kiss on her lips. "Mind you, I wouldn't consider doing anything else at 4:30 A.M."

"It's awful iffy this time of year, but we'll keep our fingers crossed. And if it's raining or the winds are too strong, we can always go back to...sleep."

"We'll just have to see," he said softly.

It was over an hour's drive from San Francisco to Napa, and it was still dark. George snuggled close to Elliot and chattered the entire way. It was just first light when they pulled into the parking lot where the balloons lifted off.

There were five other passengers, all of them tourists from out of state, and all of them excited. The captain was David Martinez, a young man who could pass for a pirate, Elliot thought, with his thick black mustache. And a pillager, he amended to himself when Martinez spotted George.

They drank coffee while the crew unrolled the huge, colorful balloon, set a powerful fan into its mouth and turned on a roaring flame to finish the job of inflating it.

"Propane?" he asked Martinez.

"Yep. That's why it's called a hot-air balloon. I'll be turning on the heat in the air and you'll feel it on the top of your head."

When the red, white and blue striped balloon was rising above them, some eighty feet into the air, they climbed into the basket.

"Hang on, Millie," George shouted to a polyester pantsuited older woman from Nebraska. "Put your foot in the opening there, and give me your hand."

The early morning air was clear and the wind slight. Elliot had wondered about turbulence, but the balloon lifted off the ground and rose so smoothly he was scarcely aware of any movement at all. They reached two thousand feet within ten minutes. It was utterly silent save for the times Martinez flipped on the propane. Napa Valley with its beautiful vineyards stretched out like a quilted spread below them. Whenever Martinez turned on the valve, flames shot upward into the balloon and hot air singed the tops of their heads. The normal air time was an hour. An hour, that is, when George wasn't along.

George and David Martinez became fast friends. He let her talk to the ground crew, called Zulu Chaser, on the radio, to tell them their likely course and altitude. They were following the balloon and would pull it safely down when it reached thirty feet or so above ground. He even let George put on his gloves and turn the valves on the propane tanks. Elliot had no doubt that Martinez would have given up a week's vacation to have brought more fuel along. As it was, they didn't have enough to cross the mountains toward the Pacific.

"It's so still," George breathed, leaning against Elliot after she'd had particularly lively conversation with the ground crew. "Not a sound."

"The birds are still asleep," Elliot said.

"How do you like your surprise?"

"You done good, kiddo, real good."

"Is this is your honeymoon?" Millie asked, eyeing them benevolently.

"Not yet," George said. "I've got to talk him into it first."

"If anybody can, it'd be you," an older man said, winking at Elliot.

They came down in the parking lot of a winery. To George's delight, the balloon was tangled in a tree for a while until the ground crew managed to pull it free.

"Happens all the time," Martinez said, unruffled as a branch poked into the basket. "Once we came down in a swimming pool. The owner wasn't too happy as I recall."

"I can't imagine that the winery owners would be pleased if you came down in the vines." Elliot said.

"I've got at least fifty stories about that," Martinez said with a reminiscent grin.

After their landing, the passengers were treated to champagne, French bread and cheese at one of the local inns in Napa.

"Just look, Elliot, my very own plaque," George said, holding up her framed Certificate of Aerostation. "Come on, hold yours up, and Drew will take our picture."

The balloon company had a photographer on hand to take pictures of the takeoff, landing, and plaque-holding.

"I need a shave," Elliot murmured out of the side of his mouth as the photographer snapped them.

"You look marvelously ferocious. Drew will send us the photos in about three weeks. Of course you'll want to frame them."

"Of course," he said.

"In your study at home or in your office?"

"We'll see."

Dr. David Thornton knocked lightly on the hospital door and stuck his head into the private room. "I've got someone for you to meet, George. Norman, here's your patient, Georgina Hathaway."

George straightened in bed and smiled at the slender man with thinning brown hair and horn-rimmed glasses. He seemed to be in his midforties, she thought, and looked terribly diffident, for a doctor. "Dr. Greenberg, a pleasure," she said, thrusting out her hand.

Norman Greenberg gulped and accepted the slender hand. He sent a wounded look toward David, who had intimated that his patient was somewhere near fifty.

"Surprised?" Elliot asked, grinning at his discomfiture.

Norman Greenberg frowned at the tall man who was standing beside his patient.

David grinned. "Norman, this is Dr. Mallory."

Norman nodded. He tried out his professional voice, but it cracked a bit. "Miss Hathaway, there's little reason to worry. I've seen your films and the whole thing should take about thirty minutes."

"How many times, Norman, have I heard your spiel?" David interrupted him with a grin.

"Now, David," George said, feeling slightly sorry for Dr. Greenberg, "I haven't heard it, and Lord knows I need lots of reassurance! Dr. Greenberg, David tells me that you have years of practice, so I have no worries about coming out of this alive. If the gentlemen will hold their tongues, you can continue."

Norman did, but it didn't sound as polished as it usually did. "How old are you?" he asked abruptly.

"Twenty-three, soon to be twenty-four," George added, with a sideways glance at Elliot.

"Ah," Norman said, investing the small word with mysterious importance.

He cleared his throat again, a habit that George found amusing, and a habit that made Elliot think contemptuously that he was a wimp.

"If I could speak to my patient," he said, "alone."

"We've been given our walking papers, Elliot," David said. "We'll be back. Just don't let him con you, George."

George was thoughtfully silent when she and Elliot were finally alone. It was ten o'clock Sunday evening, and the hospital was eerily quiet.

"This here, sweetheart, will make you sleep."

George frowned at the white pill. "You know how I feel about drugs, Elliot."

"It'll beat you lying here awake and stewing until 3:00 A.M. Take it." He watched her swallow the pill. "You'll be out of it in about ten minutes. Then I'm going home to take my own pill."

"We get started at eight o'clock," George said.

"And you'll be eating a light lunch with me at noon."

"I won't be sick?"

"Nope, at least you haven't been lying to me about your superior genes."

She gave him a wan smile. "Well, maybe it was just a little lie."

"Then I'll give you just a little lunch. We'll be playing a game of chess tomorrow night, George, I promise."

He leaned over and gathered her into his arms. "You'll be just fine, sweetheart." He held her quietly for several minutes, then kissed her lightly on her mouth.

"I'll see you bright and early tomorrow morning," he said softly, and laid her back.

"Okay," she murmured. He waited a few more minutes until he heard her breathing even into sleep, and let himself quietly out of her room.

George opened her eyes and stared straight ahead. She felt the pull of the sleeping pill, but fought it. *I should be allowed to feel my fear,* she told herself, at least for a while. She slid her hand under the covers to her belly. She would have her first scar. Dr. Greenberg had assured her it would scarcely be visible, and tried a weak joke about bikinis. She hadn't told Elliot that she had wanted to go up in the balloon yesterday because it was something she had always wanted to do before she died. Her last thought before she fell asleep was a hope that Dr. Greenberg wasn't as diffident in the operating room as he was trying to talk to her.

She would have been pleased to know that Elliot lay awake until 3:00 A.M.

George was dizzy and disoriented the next morning when a nurse woke her up to give her a tranquilizer. Elliot watched as they lifted her from her bed onto a gurney and wheeled her to the operating room. He met Maggie in the scrub room.

"You look like hell," she observed, eyeing him up and down.

"Thanks," he said dryly. "Where is our blade?"

Maggie gave him a wicked grin. "He's talking to the anesthesiologist. He's quite a ditherer, but good, Elliot, very good. So not to worry, okay? Are you going to observe?"

"I was, but I don't think so now. I'll be in my office, Maggie. Let me know the minute it's over."

"All right. It's just as well. George's friend, Dr. Hansen, asked to observe. I didn't have the heart to tell him no."

Elliot grunted in reply and left. He made coffee and fiddled with some papers on his desk. He eventually gave up trying to concentrate and waited impatiently for Lisa to come in. Her first words to him were, "Don't worry, Elliot. I've got a hot line to the OR."

"I suppose everyone in the hospital knows George is here?" He leaned back in his chair and regarded her with a resigned look.

"Probably. When you brought her in nearly a month ago, it was all over the hospital by nine o'clock the next morning that you carried in a beautiful woman in your arms dressed only in a bathrobe."

"She was in my bathrobe. I was dressed appropriately enough."

"Forgive my syntax," she said, shaking her head at him. "How was your skiing trip?"

"Fine," he said shortly.

"Don't feel like you have to make conversaion with me, Elliot. Just consider me a stick of furniture."

"Sorry, Lisa, but I'm—"

"You're worried sick," she finished for him. "Natural enough. I'll quit picking on you. Tell you what. I'll call Dr. Janis. He wants to talk to you about the NMR. Okay?"

"Why not?" Elliot said. "Lord knows how stimulating that will be."

Elliot was quite nice, if vague. When Lisa finally poked her head through the door and told him everything had gone just fine, he shot out of his chair and extended his hand to Dr. Janis. "Please excuse me. We'll speak about this again tomorrow," he said over his shoulder on his way toward the door. He stayed with George in recovery until she came to. To his bemused surprise, she was speaking French to him, and to anyone who came within earshot. At least the accent sounded French. The words made no sense, of course, and David went into peals of laughter.

"Everyone reacts differently," he said. "Once a guy was declaiming Shakespeare."

"Where's Greenberg?"

"He'll be around in a little while. He did an excellent job, Elliot. But I thought he was going to faint when the team stripped George down on the table."

"You would have to bring that up," Elliot said. "Hansen wasn't there, was he?"

"Ah, jealousy. Come on, Elliot, I was just pulling your leg. I think George is in better shape than you are."

At that moment, George started singing something that sounded like the French national anthem, and even the nurse, a stern-eyed individual, doubled over in laughter.

George recovered her wits about thirty minutes later, and the first person she recognized was Elliot. She gave him a crooked smile. "I've been cut," she said succinctly.

"And sewn back together. Any pain, George?"

She thought about it for a moment. "No. But it's the oddest thing. I know the pain's there, only I can't feel it."

"Morphine's like that."

"Something else strange, Elliot. Was there some-one in here singing songs? In French?"

He squeezed her hand. "As a matter of fact, there was. They took her back for brain surgery."

He was on the point of explaining when Dr. Green-berg walked in. He nodded curtly to Elliot and turned a beaming smile on George.

"You look pleased with yourself, doctor," George said. "You got the stitches in straight?"

"A tiny incision, Miss Hathaway, and very few stitches. Unfortunately I have to fly back to L.A. to-day. Dr. Smith will remove them next Monday." He shot a sideways glance toward Elliot, cleared his throat and said, "Do you ever visit Los Angeles, Miss Hath-away?"

"Oh, yes. Every couple of months or so."

He cleared his throat again, still looking toward El-liot, but Elliot just stared at him. "Perhaps the next time you're down, you would like to have lunch."

"A nice idea, doctor," George said in her friendli-est voice. "Thank you for coming up to take care of me."

"Not at all, Miss Hathaway. It was my pleasure."

Dr. Greenberg stretched his visit another fifteen minutes. After he had left the room, Elliot muttered, "I bet he has a wife and four kids at home."

"No," George said, twinkling at him. "He told me last night that he was divorced three years ago."

"Oh great! He's old enough to be your father!"

"True." George agreed blandly. "Quite true. Now, doctor, how about that light lunch?"

Chapter 15

It is so good to be home," George announced, squeezing Elliot tightly around his neck as he stepped into the foyer, and gazing about with immense satisfaction.

"No dashing up and down the stairs for a while, George," he said, hugging her to him. "I have a surprise for you."

"We're not at thirty-five thousand feet," she sighed. "It's bound to be a letdown."

"I can't imagine you having such a one-track mind with those stitches in your belly. No, what you need is a nurse for the next couple of days and I'm going to be it. You can order me around as much as you like."

"Good heavens," she said, startled. "Can you afford the time, Elliot?" she asked him seriously. "Really, you don't have to."

"So that's how you treat gift horses?"

"Gift stallion," she murmured in his ear.

He laughed and laid her gently on the bed. "It also means that you have to do what I tell you. Okay?"

"It's all a sham. I knew it. You want to be a dictatorial gift stallion."

"I just don't want you to be too exuberant."

"Will you sleep with me?"

"Perhaps. We'll talk about that later." He looked toward the calendar set beside the clock. Wednesday. He closed his eyes a moment. On Sunday, he'd be talking to her about important things.

"Just sleep, Elliot. You're awfully big and warm."

"I know, and you forgot cuddly," he said, forcing a smile. "How do you feel?"

"There's a little discomfort, but nothing dramatic. You really don't have to stay at home with me."

"I want to. We'll go for a short walk this afternoon so you can begin getting your strength back. On Friday, I'll race you up the stairs. You'll be at nearly a hundred percent by Monday."

"Good. Ben is agitating. He called me three times in the hospital to make sure I'd be...exuberant within the next two weeks. Braden-Tyrol has already set up the next commercial. You'll never believe it, but this one will be in a wheat field in Nebraska. I think they're going to braid my hair and have me running through the fields with Rin Tin Tin."

"Maybe you'll see Millie waving her apron at you."

"She was so sweet. She even gave me her address."

Elliot shook his head fondly.

"She...ah...wanted an invitation to our wedding," George said, watching her fingers pleat the bedspread.

Elliot said nothing. "How about some soup for lunch, kiddo? I'm hungry."

George nodded, not looking at him.

Elliot turned at the door. "I bought you some novels so you won't be climbing the walls."

"Thank you," she said, her voice expressionless.

After lunch, Elliot forced her to take another pain pill that promptly put her to sleep. He wandered into the kitchen and mechanically went through the motions of straightening up. He jumped when the phone rang.

"Yes?"

"Elliot? This is Dorothy Hathaway. I'm trying to find George. Is she there?"

Damn! "No," he lied fluently. "I believe she had a photo session this afternoon. Shall I have her call you?"

"I would appreciate it. I just wanted to tell her the news. Tod and Mariana are getting married next month here in Michigan. Mariana wants George to be her bridesmaid."

"Wonderful news, Dorothy. I'm sure George will be delighted. I will have her call you, probably this evening. She'll be here for dinner." That, at least, wasn't a bold-faced lie.

"Thank you."

They talked for some minutes longer, then Dorothy rang off. Elliot stared at the phone a minute, shrugged and walked to his study.

"I just can't get over it," George said to Elliot as they were walking down Broadway Friday afternoon. "Tod, married. I talked to Mariana yesterday, as you know, and she was calm as ever. She is the most placid, mellow person I think I've ever met. I think she'll keep Tod in line."

"A true Californian."

"Do you want to come to the wedding with me?"

Elliot looked down at his feet. "We'll see," he said finally. "You're looking great, George, and standing up straight again."

She laughed. "I kept thinking that if I did stand up straight, my stitches would pop. I can't wait to have them out." She stopped a moment and looked out over San Francisco Bay. The sky was a light blue and filled with fluffy white clouds. Scores of sailboats dotted the Bay. "Isn't it beautiful? More beautiful, I think, than the Mediterranean. They don't have San Francisco, after all."

"It helps when there's no fog."

"If it's nice tomorrow, could we go sailing?"

"If you like," he said. "Let's see how zippy you feel tomorrow morning."

Elliot never should have doubted George's zippiness. They packed a picnic lunch and were on the Bay by twelve o'clock. They docked at Angel Island, and wandered about a bit, until Elliot called a halt, and they at their lunch next to the World War II bunkers that faced the Golden Gate.

"I can always tell when you're slowing down," Elliot told her, slowing their pace down the trail back to the dock. "You stop talking."

She was silent a moment, and kicked a pebble with her sneakered toe. "Do you think I talk too much?" she asked finally.

"Don't be an ass, George," he said sharply, ruffling her hair. "That was a fond observation, not a criticism."

"There must be something about me you don't like," she said hopefully. "Something you'd like to change?"

"Hmmm," he said. "Let me cogitate on that. I'm sure there's at least a dozen things, but at the moment, I'm sated on food and sailing. My critical brain is at rest." He didn't mean to say anything more, but the words came out without his permission. "And what would you like to change in me?"

You're evasive as hell and I don't know what you're thinking. "Well, you're awfully smooth."

He cocked a black brow at her. "What does that mean?"

"You're always very controlled."

His eyes crinkled in laughter. "You mean like the time at Aspen when I played the caveman and embarrassed the hell out of both of us?"

"You're right. Maybe I should find another word. Although," she added thoughtfully, "that was the first time I've ever seen you do something that made you uncomfortable. Most of the time, unlike me, you think before you act or say something."

"I've had quite a number of years to learn that I can usually avoid making a fool of myself if I exercise a bit of thought before opening my big mouth."

"So you believe that by the time I've reached your exalted years, I'll be wise enough to keep my mouth shut?"

"Something like that," he said easily. "Look at the cormorant, George."

Evasive as hell, she thought, but dutifully gave her attention to the long-necked bird preening on top of a piling.

When they reached Elliot's house, George gave him no arguments and snuggled into bed for a nap before dinner. She hated feeling fatigued. It made her feel somehow not in control of herself. She awoke much refreshed, but was careful to conserve her energy during the evening. They watched TV for an hour, George in her usual place on the floor with her back against the sofa, between Elliot's legs. She tilted her head back at ten o'clock. "You even look handsome upside down," she said, grinning at him. "No, don't say it," she added, holding up her hand. "You've had years to perfect that pose."

"Okay, kiddo, I won't say it. You ready for bed?"

She nodded, and quickly lowered her head so he wouldn't see the gleam in her eyes. "Are you coming up now too?" She smiled at her normal tone. He had treated her like a sexless patient all week.

"Yeah," he said, helping her to her feet. "I guess so."

"I think I'll take a shower," she said matter-of-factly.

"Be sure not to get your stitches wet."

Elliot was reading one of his medical journals in bed when she came out of the bathroom, scrubbed and wearing a blue flannel granny gown. She gave a convincing yawn and slipped into bed.

"I hope you didn't overdo it today," Elliot said. "You make me forget that you were in surgery five days ago."

"Yes," she said, "but don't forget that I'm a woman, and women have more endurance than men."

"I never should have shown you that article," he said, and turned out the light.

She leaned over and he gave her his usual sexless kiss good-night. Very slowly, she wriggled out of her nightgown.

"Are you having trouble getting settled?" he asked.

"Oh no, I'll be perfectly settled in just a moment." She eased over and pressed herself against his side. She heard him take a sharp breath. She rose on her elbow and pressed her breasts against his naked chest.

"George," he began.

She eased her leg over his belly. "You can't escape me now, Dr. Mallory," she whispered, and clasping his face between her hands, she kissed him.

He felt her smooth thigh rubbing lightly over his belly, and despite all his noble intentions his body reacted swiftly.

"No," he said into her mouth. "No, George."

He clasped her shoulders, wanting to pull her away, but he felt her soft breasts against his chest, and his control slipped.

"I feel perfectly marvelous and I want you, Elliot. Please."

But I don't want to feel like a perfect louse!

Her tongue slipped between his lips, and instead of pushing her away, he drew her closer.

One last time, damn it, one last time, George.

Her hand gently closed around him, and he heard a rough groan in his own throat. He hated himself as he turned toward her and pushed her gently onto her back. "George," he tried one last time, "I don't want to hurt you."

"If you are my gift stallion," she whispered, "then for tonight, you'll do what I like."

"Damn it," he said roughly. "It's been so damned long." He kissed her fiercely, and his hands roved down her body. She felt his fingertips lightly probing her, and she was lost to the sensation of his touch. When he lifted her over him, he shuddered as he entered her, but he teased her, holding her about her waist, not letting her feel him completely.

"Please," she whispered.

Then he was filling her, caressing her with his fingers, drawing her forward to kiss her breasts.

Her body convulsed as she reached her climax, and her soft keening cries filled the silence. It took all his control to hold off his own release. "I love you," she cried, and sobbed softly into his shoulder. He felt twisted with guilt, but his body ignored his mind, and he exploded deep inside her.

"Jesus," he groaned some moments later. He eased her forward until she lay full length on top of him. He was still deep within her, and when he tried to move, she held her body rigid. He could feel her heart pounding against him, and a light sheen of sweat covered her.

"I thought I was going to die," she said, her voice still shaking slightly. "In fact, it's still a close thing."

He stroked her back, soothing her, wishing the simple movement of his hands would soothe him as well.

"I'm too tired to move," she said, sighing deeply.

"Then you can be my blanket tonight." He paused a moment, aware finally of the bandage on her belly. "I didn't hurt you, did I?"

"I will only be hurt if you leave me," she said.

"I'm only a man, George. You know, no endurance."

"No staying power?" she asked, moving sensuously over him.

To his chagrin, he felt himself growing hard again within her.

"That's nice," she murmured, and saved him by falling asleep, her cheek nestled in the hollow of his throat.

He lay awake for a long time, staring up at the darkened ceiling. "Some control, you randy bastard," he muttered, his voice filled with anger at himself.

George awoke, a soft smile in her eyes and on her lips. She reached for Elliot, but she was alone in bed. She propped herself up on her elbow and gazed toward the alarm clock.

"Good heavens," she said aloud. It was nearly eleven o'clock. She hummed softly as she showered. To her surprise, clothes were laid out for her on the bed when she emerged from the bathroom.

"Thank you," she called downstairs, and giggled at the knee socks Elliot had picked out. They were white wool, covered with red cabbage roses.

She felt marvelously happy, and was still humming when she made her way downstairs.

Elliot emerged from the kitchen, and she stood staring at him for a long moment. He was wearing brown corduroy jeans and a ribbed turtleneck sweater. "Forget what I said about your control," she said, smiling at him. "You're perfect just the way you are."

He didn't meet her eyes, and she cocked her head to one side in silent question.

"Come on in the kitchen," he said finally. "I've made you some pancakes and bacon."

Whenever George felt uncertain, she chattered. "I weighed myself and I'm down a pound. Lots of pancakes, if you please. Oh, and the bacon is perfect, crispy, just as I like it."

Elliot smiled painfully, but did not interrupt her. He sat down at the table and drank a cup of coffee, watching her eat.

"...So if you really don't mind, doctor, I think I'll forgo a five-mile jog today. I hear there's a new exhibit at the museum, but the aquarium's always fun. Maybe—"

He felt a cold sweat on his forehead. He knew she sensed there was something wrong. He found himself memorizing the sound of her voice, the way she lilted upward at the end of a sentence.

"So what do you think, Elliot?"

He looked up, studying her face. He forced himself to smile and it felt like his face was cracking. "Are you finished eating?"

She nodded and patted her stomach. "I wish you'd teach me how to fix pancakes like yours."

"It's not hard. You read the directions on the box." Jesus, he sounded like a cold bastard. He rose from his chair. "George, would you please come into the living room?"

He saw her glance at him warily, and quickly strode out of the kitchen. She followed him, sat on the edge of the sofa and proffered him a mock salute. "Yes, sergeant major?"

He drew a deep breath. "We must talk, George."

He ran his hand through his hair. Damn, he thought, furious with himself, furious with the situation. "I can't marry you, George," he said abruptly.

There was utter silence. George felt as though she had been punched in the stomach. Yet she wasn't surprised, not really. She heard herself ask, quite clamly, "May I ask why?"

"There are several reasons," he said in a clipped voice. "I think the most important reason is the most obvious. You are twenty-three—"

"Almost twenty-four," she interrupted him.

"And I will be thirty-nine at the end of the year. There are fifteen years separating us, George. That's a lot of years, too many. You are not of my generation, or I am not of yours, however you want to look at it. If you have any memories at all of the sixties, they're doubltess of playing sports with your brothers."

"I grew up in the sixties."

"No, you were a child in the sixties, not an adult. Don't you understand that I was in high school when you were born? I could have baby-sat for you."

George fought back the cold dread his words brought her. She had an odd feeling, as if a prison door was closing on her. She smiled at him and said calmly, with a hint of humor, "Elliot, you act as though I'm an unthinking child, like I don't know what I want, like I'm not mature enough to make decisions about my life. The fifteen years mean nothing to me. I have never noticed that you were hesitant to talk to me about anything. I always thought that was a very important part of marriage: two people enjoying each other's company, sharing ideas and, well, playing together. Have I been deluding myself? Don't you enjoy my company?"

"Yes, I enjoy your company, but we've only known each other for six months, George."

"So you think I'm going to turn boring on you because I don't remember John Kennedy? What does that have to do with us?"

"It's more the difference in our experiences." He heard the growing tension in his voice. What had he expected, anyway? For George to fold up her tent and leave him without any discussion? "George, most of my friends are my age or older. Take David and Doris. They could be your parents, for God's sake."

"I doubt they'd like to hear you say that."

"Probably not, yet it's nearly true. But the facts remain the facts, George."

"I assure you that if I were thirty-eight and you were twenty-three, I would feel the same."

He was forced to smile, but shook his head at the same time. "Perhaps, back in Victorian times, it would have been all right for a husband to be much older than his wife. But not today, George. You don't want to spend your life with a man who will be fifty when you're thirty-five. Thirty-five, I might add, is still younger than I am now."

"So," she said slowly, here eyes locking with his, "you're making the decision for me, and I really haven't any say in the matter?"

He drew a deep breath. "Yes," he said.

"It means so little to you that I love you? That I want to spend my life with you?"

She saw a muscle jerk in his jaw. "George," he said quietly, "I took advantage of your youth, your inexperience. No, don't interrupt me. Admittedly, it was you who picked me, and as you said, you picked me because I was older and you trusted me to introduce you to sex. I knew what would happen, George. You didn't. You became infatuated with me. First love and all that."

George sprang up from the sofa. "Infatuated with you? That is the most conceited, ridiculous thing I've ever heard you say! Damn you, Elliot Mallory, I am not stupid. Give me some credit for knowing the difference between infatuation and love."

He chose to ignore her words. "Listen to me," he said sharply. "It is natural, if the man isn't a total clod, for a woman who is sexually innocent to become enamored with him if sex between them is satisfying. George, I'm the only man you've ever slept with. I, on the other hand, have slept with many women."

She gasped, and tears stung her eyes. She flung out her hands, silently begging him to stop. "So you just think of me as a satisfactory lay? Until someone better comes along?"

"Now you *are* being stupid. Just as I experimented when I was your age, it's natural for you to experiment now. You no longer have any need of me. It's time for you to discover men much closer to your own age. And when you finally find a man you want to marry, you will do it with proper experience—"

"Now you're sounding like a bloody computer!"

"George, I have enjoyed our six months together. You can't believe that knowing you has meant nothing to me. But I will not take any more advantage of you than I already have. Not only are you very young, you have an unbelievable future in front of you." He sighed and ran his hand distractedly through his hair. "That's probably the most important reason. You will doubtless be a celebrity within a short time. You have a new and exciting life ahead of you. I cannot be a part of that, nor will I trap you into a marriage that you would likely find stifling within a year."

"You have thought this all through quite completely, haven't you?" she asked slowly.

"Yes."

She tried for sarcasm, but fell short. "How shocked you must have been when I asked you to marry me! I imagine that sort of crass behavior on the part of a woman didn't happen in your generation?"

"Probably not."

"You're a big boy, doctor, and I'm sure you got over the shock quickly enough. Why didn't you tell me you wouldn't marry me when I asked you two weeks ago?"

He couldn't meet her eyes.

"Oh, my God! How stupid can you get?" She laughed, a raw, hoarse sound that made him wince. "You put me off because you were afraid I wouldn't have the operation! You believed I was so infantile, so uncaring about myself, that I would be devastated by your rejection and kill myself. Well, damn you, answer me!"

"Yes," he said, "I was concerned about your surgery."

"I don't believe you, I really don't. What a fool you must think I am. And here I've had the nerve to interrupt your precious, prepared speech! Well, are you through with your speech? Can I now say something without you ignoring me?"

"I heard your comments, George."

"But they weren't important enough to respond to?"

"I've responded as best as I can."

"You self-righteous bastard!" she yelled at him. "Aren't you worried that I won't have my stitches taken out? I wonder why you didn't wait to give me my walking papers until tomorrow."

"Stop it, George!" he roared back at her. "I am doing what I believe best for both of us. If I've gone about it unwisely, then I am sorry. But, George, you must believe me. Infatuation doesn't last. Lord knows the first girls I made love with I swore I wanted to spend my life with. It's simply not true. It doesn't last."

Her legs felt suddenly wobbly, and she sank down onto the sofa. "There is something I must know."

"Yes?"

"Do you love me?"

He glanced away, his lips tightening. She wanted to scream at him, yell at him, but all she said was, "No, don't say it. I guess I can stand to hear most things, but not that." No, she thought, he couldn't love her, at least not as she did him.

What are you going to say now, you clod? "I care very much about you, George," he said very calmly, "but that really has no bearing on anything. It's time for you to enjoy your success, without me hanging about your neck. And perhaps soon you'll be ready to go out with other men, younger men who are in your business. You will find the right man for you, George, a man of your own generation, and I, well, I will find myself more at ease with women closer to my age."

"Like Eileen Raeburn?"

"Yes, like Eileen."

"I suppose there's nothing more to say, is there?"

He could hear the tears in her voice, and the pain. *I am doing the right thing*, he told himself yet again.

"No. I packed up all your things."

She broke into wild laughter. "I wondered why you laid out my clothes! Everything else was sitting next to the front door!"

"I will take you home now."

"I wouldn't go to the corner with you," she said. She walked swiftly toward the front door, and flung over her shoulder, "Thank you for the educational experience, Dr. Mallory. I'm certain with you style, you'll have another woman in your bed quite soon to keep you warm."

"George, I'm driving you home."

"Go to hell," she said quite clamly, wrapping her pride around her, and slammed the front door behind her.

Elliot stood very quiet for several moments. Then he walked to the entrance hall, picked up her two suitcases and strode to his car. He drove slowly, watching for her. He finally pulled up across from her house, carried her suitcases to her front porch, then returned to his car and waited. Fifteen minutes later, he saw her walking to her front door. Her shoulders were slumped forward, and her head was bowed. He watched her pause at the sight of her luggage, then unlock the door. She kicked the suitcases inside, and without a backward glance, walked inside and closed the door behind her.

He drove slowly home, feeling like an old man.

Chapter 16

Dr. David Thornton gazed thoughtfully down at the people six stories below his office. He saw Dr. Margaret Smith stop Elliot. They were likely talking about the weather, David imagined. Elliot would allow nothing more. And it had been six months. He shook his head and returned to his desk. Ten minutes later, Maggie knocked lightly on his door and stepped into his office.

"How are you, Maggie?" He waved her to a chair.

"I'll survive, which is better than I can say for one of my friends."

"I saw you talking to Elliot," he remarked, twirling a pencil between his fingers.

"Yes, briefly. He'd just come back from his daily swim. I'm beginning to wonder if he is even a friend anymore."

"It's been six months," David said. He sat down in his swivel chair, leaned his head back against the soft leather, and closed his eyes. "You know, I remember distinctly being furious with George for dumping him. After all, she is the beautiful young thing rushing headlong into fame, meeting exciting people and getting rid of excess baggage. I believe at the time I was tempted to put a contract out on her for treating Elliot like that. Then one of the radiology residents, a friend of hers, let it slip that it was Elliot who had done the dumping." He sighed deeply. "I couldn't believe it."

"You and everyone else! Incidentally, the resident's name is Randy Hansen, and he told me that, too."

David opened his eyes long enough to send her an admiring glance. "Good for you, Maggie. I was too much of a chicken to check it out for myself."

"Elliot must be crazy."

"Well, if he wasn't crazy when he tossed her over, he is now. He's lost weight, he's as mean as any dictator and he's refused every invitation Doris has sent him."

"And there's not a thing we can do about it," Maggie moaned. "I tried to talk to him once, a couple of months ago. Boy, did I regret it. He didn't yell at me or anything like that, he just froze up. I felt like I was next to an ice float in the Antarctic."

"Well, he treats me like a well-meaning lad who doesn't know better. I haven't seen any new commercials lately on TV. I wonder what George is up to?"

It was a purely rhetorical remark, and Maggie only shrugged. "If you come up with a bright idea, count me in. How much longer will he continue the way he is?"

"Lord knows. I don't. I guess we might as well discuss something we can do something about. What about the Winthrop woman? What did the scan show?"

They were still involved in discussing Mrs. Winthrop when David's secretary, Mary Carson, stuck her head in his office. "Your wife is here to see you, Dr. Thornton. She says it's urgent."

David was out of his chair in an instant. Doris never came uninvited to the hospital unless something catastrophic had happened.

"David!" Doris stopped short until she recognized Maggie. She turned and closed the office door.

"What's the matter? Are the kids all right?"

"The kids are great," Doris said. "And soon Elliot Mallory will be too. Maggie, how are you? Come here, you two," she continued without a pause. "Take a look at this!"

"A fashion magazine?" David said, bewildered.

Doris flipped through the pages. "Wait a minute," she said, a smug smile on her face."

Maggie gasped. "Dear Lord!"

David scratched his head. "I believe," he said slowly, a look of unholy glee on his face, "that Elliot Mallory's day is not going to end the way it began."

"He'd have to be dead!"

Ten minutes later, David entered Elliot's office on the third floor, the fashion magazine tucked under his arm. "Hi, Lisa. Is your boss busy?"

Lisa Dickerson rolled her eyes heavenward. "He's working on a lecture now. He demolished two residents this morning and bawled me out when he got back from swimming. Are you sure you want to see him?"

"You bet your life I want to see him!" He headed toward Elliot's office. He turned and smiled smugly. "Just hang around a few minutes, Lisa. I'll bet you one hundred dollars you're going to see a vast change in your boss."

"Sure, and Tom Selleck is going to walk into my life!"

"Just you wait," David said, tapped on the closed door and opened it.

Lisa heard Elliot snap, "What is it you want, David?"

I think, Dr. Thornton, she thought sadly, *you're going to lose your hundred dollars.*

"Good afternoon, Elliot. Fine day, isn't it? No fog, unusual for July."

Elliot ran his hand through his hair. "What is it, David? I'm busy."

"You're going to be even busier shortly."

"Look, David. I am busy, and I don't have time for your cryptic wit."

"I brought you something. Here, take a look." David handed Elliot the fashion magazine, opening it up to a double-page color spread.

Elliot shot David an impatient glance, and looked down at the pages.

"*Oh my God!*"

"Yes," David agreed pleasantly. "I thought something along those same lines, I think."

Elliot stared down at George, smiling in at least a dozen different poses, modeling a different outfit in each. She looked utterly beautiful. And very pregnant. His hands shook. The pictures showed her in all stages of her pregnancy.

He swallowed painfully. "Where did you get this?"

"Doris brought it in a few minutes ago."

"How—far along is she, David?"

David studied the photos. "About six months I'd say."

A look of intense pain crossed Elliot's face. "I didn't know. She didn't tell me."

"Obviously. But now you do know."

David observed a blazing transformation in the next few seconds. Elliot's eyes gleamed purposefully, and he straightened to his full height, a grim smile on his face. "I owe you one, David," he said abruptly. "Now, if you'll excuse me..."

He grabbed his suit jacket and headed toward the door.

"Good luck," David called after him.

"Well," Lisa said when David joined her in her office, "I'm glad I didn't accept your bet! What happened? He told me he'd likely be taking off the rest of the week."

David grinned, handed Lisa the magazine and strode whistling to the door.

"Glory be!"

He was still grinning when he reached his office.

Elliot rang the doorbell, then pounded on the door.

He heard George's voice, and felt a rush of excitement. "Who is it?"

What if she refused to let him in? He gritted his teeth. He'd kick the damned door down. "It's Elliot. Open the door, George."

He heard the chain fall and the lock click open. The door opened slowly, and Elliot quickly pushed it further open and stepped inside.

He stared at her for a long moment, a slow smile spreading over his face. "Hello, George," he said. "You're looking...somewhat different."

Actually, he thought, she looked dreadful, if such a thing was possible for George. She was wearing a floor-length pink robe that molded around her protruding stomach. Her hair looked lank and dull and was pulled back in a ratty ponytail. She wasn't wearing any makeup, and her face was pale, her eyes puffy. He wanted more than anything to pull her into his arms, but he stood quietly, watching her. He didn't know what to expect, but her sugar-sweet voice took him aback.

"Elliot Mallory, as I live and breathe. Do come in, doctor. Don't tell me the establishment is reduced to making house calls?"

She didn't await his response, but turned on her heel and headed slowly into the living room. She looked like a small ship whose sails weren't quite keeping her balanced. He thrust out his hand when she listed sharply to the left, and dropped it back to his side when she righted.

· "No," he said agreeably, following her, "I've come to see you."

"How very pleasant," she murmured, carefully easing herself down into an easy chair. She hefted herself up again. "How rude of me. Would you care for something to drink, doctor?"

"It's too early," Elliot said.

She gave him a faint, mocking smile and disappeared into the kitchen. He stayed on her heels. The kitchen was spotless, save for empty wine bottles sticking out of a garbage bag in front of the sink cabinets. He watched, astonished and dismayed, as George opened the refrigerator and took out a bottle of wine. She raised it to him in a salute. "Are you certain you won't join me?"

He shook his head.

She poured a glassful of white wine. A water glass, he thought, a frown deepening on his forehead. She raised it to her lips and drank a full third of the glass.

She clutched the bottle in one hand, the glass in the other, and walked past him back into the living room. She eased down into an easy chair. To his further astonishment, she lit a cigarette, drew on it deeply and blew out a vague smoke ring.

He noticed an overflowing ashtray on the table beside her.

"Do sit down, doctor," she said, waving toward the couch. "Perhaps you'll be kind enough to tell me why you're here. It is a weekday, you know, and such an important person as yourself has so many demands on his time.''

"George," he said softly, "why didn't you tell me?"

"I take it you saw the layout in the magazine?"

He nodded. "Why didn't you tell me?" he repeated.

George tossed down another long drink of wine. She lowered her glass and smiled at him very sweetly. "Why ever should I have told you about my... condition?"

"I think that would be obvious!"

"Oh," she said, as if in surprise. "You think this is your child? An understandable mistake, I suppose," she continued, nodding patiently at him. "But you needn't worry, doctor. This one isn't yours."

"Stop this, George! You know you should have told me immediately."

"Now, now," she said in a mock-soothing voice, "don't start feeling guilty. I'm not going to sue you for paternity." She paused a moment, frowning thoughtfully. "In fact, even if I wanted to sue some man, I wouldn't know who it should be."

"What the hell does that mean? You're six months pregnant. That means you conceived in February."

"No, you're wrong. I'm only a little over five months along. The baby is just big, that's all. And, as I said, you're not the father." She took another drink of wine.

"When did you stop working?" he asked abruptly.

"Let's see," she said, pursing her pale lips. "Today is Wednesday. I guess my last day was Friday. Yes, Friday."

Thank God, he thought to himself. The drinking and smoking had been going on for less than a week; at least he prayed so.

He stared a moment at her stomach. "Don't lie to me, George. I know you have every right to be angry, but—"

She interrupted him with a shrill laugh. "Angry? With you, doctor? Your conceit is showing again. You were quite right, you know. When I was in Nebraska in the wheat fields, I met the nicest man. He was directing the commercial. A much younger man than you. No more than thirty, and very much of my generation. We became quite chummy. He was nearly as good a lover as you. He could be the father, I suppose." She appeared to give it considerable thought, then shook her head. "But you see, then I was in New York, with Damien. He's not a terribly large man, so I'm not sure whether the child could be his." She patted her round stomach. "I guess I'll just have to wait and see who the kid looks like. Lord, I do hope he or she doesn't take after Norman Greenberg! Although," she added, her eyes lighting in fond memory, "it was a lovely weekend with him in Los Angeles."

He didn't believe her, not for a second. He wished he could shake her and hold her at the same time. His child, he thought, his child, and he hadn't known. "Who is your doctor?" he asked, his voice oddly sharp.

He watched her light another cigarette.

"You have seen a doctor?"

She blew smoke toward him. "I really don't see that it's any of you concern, doctor."

He clasped his hands tightly in his lap.

"You appear to have this mistaken notion that, without you, I'm quite helpless," she remarked indifferently. "Perhaps in your generation women are supposed to be ninnies who can't function without a strong man about? Don't kid yourself, doctor."

He watched her stub out her cigarette and immediately light another. Her hands were shaking.

"No," he said, his eyes still on her hands, "I never thought you in the least helpless. You must have gotten pregnant that last night we were together," he added without a pause.

"My, but you still refuse to listen to me or believe me, don't you?" She shrugged elaborately. "That's nothing new. I should have remembered that once you made up your mind about something, nothing could change it, especially not a flighty postteenager. In any case, doctor, I have nothing more to say to you. I do apologize for the magazine layout. I imagine that it must have given you a moment's pause. But you're off the hook now. No more guilt. Do you mind showing yourself out?"

He wanted nothing more than to take her in his arms. Instead, he nodded, and rose.

"It was very noble of you to come by," she said, anger spilling into her voice. "Needless to say I hope I never have to see you again. Oh, incidentally, that was a lovely wedding present you sent to Mariana and Tod. I thought myself that a giant toad would have been more appropriate, but then again, what do I know?''

"Goodbye, George," he said. He did not pause, but strode quickly out of the living room and the house. He closed the door very quietly.

George swilled down the rest of the wine in her glass. A bitter smile crossed her lips. He was gone. Forever. It was over now, for good. Well, what had she expected? She reached for the wine bottle and tilted it to her mouth. She didn't care; damn him, she wouldn't care.

Two hours later, at four o'clock in the afternoon, there was another knock on George's front door. She stared bleary-eyed toward the obnoxious sound. She heaved herself slowly out of the chair and walked in a weaving line toward the front door.

"Who is it?"

There was a pause, and then a low, gruff voice. "Miss Hathaway? A telegram for you."

Telegram. Someone was ill. She felt fear clutch at her, and quickly opened the door. Elliot stood before her. She tried to slam the door in his face, but she was clumsy and slow, and he pushed back and strode into the entrance hall.

"Get out!" she yelled at him. "You lying...toad!"

"You can call me every name in the book if it will make you feel better. Come on, George, let's get you packed."

She stared him, blinking vaguely. "Packed," she repeated stupidly. "What are you talking about?"

"I'm going to dry you out, sweetheart. Lord, but you're drunk."

"Stay away from me, Elliot Mallory!" She backed away from him, her hands splayed in front of her to ward him off. "The child isn't yours, for God's sake! Get out!"

"While you're cursing me, you can also tell me more about all your lovers," he said calmly. "Come on, let's go get your things together."

Rage bubbled up inside her. Six months of hurt and loneliness. She flew at him, striking him with her fists, sobbing her fury.

Elliot caught her against his chest and gently held her arms to her sides. "Forgive me, sweetheart," he whispered against her temple.

Suddenly she became very still.

"George?"

She raised her face. "I'm going to be sick," she gasped. She wriggled out of his grasp and lurched clumsily toward the bathroom. She made it, barely.

She didn't have the strength to fight him. He helped her down to her knees and held her while she lost all the wine she had consumed. She moaned softly, wishing she could die.

"No," she whispered as he picked her up in his arms and carried her into her bedroom. He laid her gently down and straightened over her. "Just lie still. I'll be right back."

Elliot laid a damp washcloth over her forehead. "Take these," he said, and lifted her slightly. She swallowed the pills. "Now wash your mouth out. It'll make you feel better."

She gargled with the mouthwash, felt her stomach knot again and moaned softly as she spit it into the glass he held.

"I don't believe this," she muttered.

"I know." He couldn't either, actually. The sight of George drunk and then vilely sick shook him. And it was his fault, all of it.

"What are you doing here?"

"We're going to Carmel."

George tried to struggle to a sitting position, but found it an impossibility and fell ignominiously back onto the pillow. "Like hell we are," she spat at him, jerking off the damp washcloth. "I wouldn't go to heaven with you!"

"You have no choice. Now hush."

She was beginning to feel drowsy. "What were those pills?"

Something to make you more docile. "Just something to settle your stomach. Concentrate on getting your bearings again, George. Everything will be all right, I promise you."

"Nothing will ever be all right," she said bitterly. "Your promises aren't worth the breath you say them with." *But he never made any promises to you, did he, you fool? Not one.*

She heard him moving about her bedroom. If only she didn't feel so wretched, she thought, she could get up and kick him out. Damn him!

Elliot smiled as he folded several pair of her more outrageous knee socks into a suitcase. But her underwear very nearly undid him. Gone were the silky, very sexy bikini panties and in their place were sensible, full-cut cotton ones. Her bras brought a brief smile to his lips. Not only were they noble in size, they were Puritan white, just like the panties. He felt an overpowering sadness at what he had done, and he prayed it could be undone. He packed her clothes methodically, looking every few minutes toward the bed. She was nearly asleep. So much the better, he thought. He couldn't imagine carrying her kicking and screaming to his car. He left the house very quietly, and locked her suitcase in the trunk.

When he returned, he leaned over her to be sure that she was asleep, and gently lifted her in his arms. She stirred and muttered in an angry, slurred voice, "Put me down, you jerk! I'm not going anywhere with you."

"It's all right, sweetheart," he said softly. He felt the baby move, and clasped her more tightly against his chest. He carried her to the car, gently settled her on the front seat and unfolded a blanket over her.

She slept the whole way to Carmel, her cheek pillowed on his thigh. It was nearing sunset when he pulled the car into the parking lot of the Brittany Inn. He had managed to book the same room he and George had had eight months before. Elliot left her asleep in the car and quickly took care of the registration.

George awoke abruptly when he laid her on the bed in their room. She stared up at him, confusion in her eyes. "I—don't understand," she began, trying to sit up.

"We're at the Brittany Inn. I brought some orange juice. Would you like some? It'll help settle your stomach."

His very professional tone made her scowl, but she eagerly accepted the juice. She drank two glasses without pause. She leaned back against the pillows and watched him silently as he unpacked the suitcases. She wished she didn't feel so bloody tired, so bloody helpless.

"Would you like to have a bath?" he asked her, once he had finished putting their clothing away. "I brought shampoo, your dryer and anything else you'll need."

She said nothing, but let her scowl deepen.

"After you've bathed, we'll have dinner here in our room," he continued evenly. "No wine."

"Bastard," she muttered under her breath.

He only grinned at her. "All right," she said, realizing she hadn't washed her hair in four days. Her scalp itched.

"Good," he said briskly. "I'll run the water for you. Just stay put for a minute."

She was leaning against the bathroom sink when he straightened over the tub. He much preferred her anger to the look of utter defeat in her eyes.

"Would you like me to help you into the tub?"

He reached toward the zipper on her robe, but she slapped his hands away. "I don't need your help, Dr. Mallory," she snapped at him. "I don't need anything from you!"

His eyes caressed her belly. "It looks like you've already gotten quite a bit from me," he said.

She glared at him.

"Soak a while. It'll rejuvenate your mind after the pills I gave you. You're no challenge at all as you are."

She clutched a tube of toothpaste and flung it at him, but he ducked it and let himself out of the bathroom.

Chapter 17

There was a rerun of *Star Trek* on TV. Elliot left it on.
He wanted George to eat and was afraid that without
the distraction, she wouldn't.

He heard a knock on the door over the whine of her
hair dryer in the bathroom. A fresh-faced waiter
wheeled in a cart of food. Elliot made innocuous
conversation with him, tipped him and closed the door
after him.

"George," he called. "Dinner's here. Spaghetti
with clam sauce and lots of garlic bread."

The bathroom door opened and George came out,
looking much better than before. Nothing like a bath
to soak out evil humors, he thought. Her hair was
nearly dry, soft and silky about her face. She was
wearing a clean nightgown and robe. She paused uncertainly.

He smiled, pulled out a chair next to a small table and said matter-of-factly, "If you like, you can watch Captain Kirk while you're eating. I think it's the one with the woman Romulan commander who falls in love with Spock."

"The cloaking device," she said, sitting down. "The woman, of course, loses out in the end," she added in a wintry voice.

He refused to be drawn. "I ordered some more orange juice for you."

"Thank you," she said.

Elliot was thankful for Kirk and Spock. By the end of the show, George had polished off nearly all her spaghetti and was munching on the last of the garlic bread. She had drunk all the orange juice.

Elliot rose, straightened the dishes on the tray and wheeled it outside to the landing. "I'm going to take a shower now," he said when he returned.

She started and turned wide eyes to him. He watched her tongue slide over her bottom lip.

"What's the matter?" he asked gently.

He saw her gaze flick toward the bed, and understood.

"Where are you going to sleep?" she blurted out.

"George," he said very calmly, "we are going to sleep in that bed. I have no intention of ravishing you. Would you like to sleep now?"

She nodded, clutched the arms of the chair and pushed herself up. He wanted to smile at her awkwardness. It seemed that she was still trying to find her new center of gravity. Once she was standing, facing him, she drew a deep breath. "I want to leave tomorrow. I don't want to stay here with you."

He looked at her thoughtfully, searching for the right words to say to her.

"Damn you! I don't want your pity!"

He blinked at her. "Pity," he repeated.

"I told you the child isn't yours Elliot. I don't know what game you're playing, but I'm not going along with it."

"Sit down," he said.

"Don't you give me orders, you cold-blooded jerk!"

"Sit down, George." He strode toward her, and George plunked back down into the chair. He stopped at the chair opposite her, and clutched at its back until his knuckles whitened. "Now you will listen for a minute," he said evenly. "You will stop lying about the baby. And you will tell me why you didn't call me the instant you found out you were pregnant."

"Why?" she asked, her voice cold. "So you could offer to pay for an abortion? So you could accuse me of getting pregnant on purpose to trap you into marriage?"

"You honestly believed I would want you to have an abortion?" he asked quietly.

She shrugged. "It didn't matter, really. By the time I realized I was pregnant, it was too late anyway. God knows I wish it hadn't been!"

He closed his eyes a moment to gain control. He understood her anger and her distrust of him, and searched for the right words to say to her.

"What's the matter, doctor? Does the thought of being a father distress you so much? It needn't. The child is mine, and mine alone. I will swear I've slept with every man in San Francisco if you try for custody rights!"

He ignored her spate of words and locked his gaze on her face. "Do you really believe, George—no, don't look away from me—that I would have thought about, much less suggested, an abortion? Or thought that you had gotten pregnant on purpose?"

She pushed the hair off her forehead, and shrugged. "Why not? I thought I knew you, but obviously I was wrong. When Randy Hansen came to see me in March, to accuse *me* of kissing you off, I realized how smooth you are, doctor. And I was a fool. But even fools learn. Now, if you will excuse me, I am tired."

"You knew it was likely I would see you pregnant in that fashion magazine. Did you think I would ignore the situation?"

"No, I thought you would likely call me. In fact, I was looking forward to it, knowing that at the very least you'd feel guilty as hell. I suppose men of your age would, even though I'm only a flighty model. But you came to my house, so terribly controlled and so forceful. It makes no difference, Elliot. None at all."

"We'll see about that," he said.

He saw her hands clench into fists, then open again. "There is nothing further to see about," she said, and rose from her chair. He said nothing more. Once she was in bed, he turned out the lights and went into the bathroom. He showered quickly, worried she would try to sneak away.

She didn't move when he slipped into bed beside her. He stared for a moment into the darkness, then rose again. He lowered the thermostat to fifty degrees and returned to bed, a smile on his lips.

When he awoke at dawn, he lay very still. George was snuggled against him, her body curved against his back, her arm flung over his chest. The feel of her new shape delighted him, and he wanted nothing more than to roll her over and caress her belly, to feel his child within her. Very carefully, he eased onto his side to face her. He drew her into his arms, and fell back to sleep with an occasional feather kick of the child against his stomach.

George emerged slowly from a pleasant dream, aware that she was toasty warm. She stiffened, aware that she was molded against the length of Elliot's body, her face nestled against his chest. Her nightgown had ridden up a bit, and his bare legs were pressed against hers. She tried to wriggle away from him without waking him, but succeeded only in making him tighten his arms around her. He murmured softly, whether in his sleep or not she didn't know, "Go back to sleep. The alarm hasn't gone off yet."

So long, she thought, it had been so long. Her pride and rage had fought against her misery for a while, but even they had faltered, and she had felt like a brittle, fallen autumn leaf, crushed headlessly underfoot. Had she really expected him to merely telephone her when he saw the magazine? No, she finally admitted to herself. She had known he would come; she had wanted him to come to her. What would he do now? More important, what would she do? She felt tears sting her eyes and gulped them back.

"Good morning."

She froze in midstretch at the sound of his soft voice.

"What time is it?" she blurted out, holding very still.

"Nearly nine o'clock, and time for breakfast. Did you sleep well?"

Elliot allowed her to pull away from him. "Yes, I guess so, but it got so cold."

"Yes, it did," he agreed smoothly.

"I have to go to the bathroom," George said after a couple of moments of silence.

"Do you feel all right?" he asked as she climbed over him.

"Of course," she said sharply. "I'm not sick!"

"I hope you stay obnoxiously healthy." He paused a moment, dropping his eyes to her stomach. "You look beautiful, George."

She stared at him a moment, aware that her hair was a tangled mess around her face and that she was swathed from neck to toe in a blue flannel granny gown. "Sure," she said, curling her lips at him, "and a swan has a short neck!"

His laughter followed her into the bathroom.

"Are you ready?" Elliot asked.

George nodded. She was wearing a gray wool jumper with a pale pink silk blouse and low heeled shoes, and her hair was pulled back with a gold clip.

"Will you believe me if I tell you you look very nice this morning?"

"You're into gray tents, are you?"

He gently clasped her shoulders and turned her toward the mirror. "Why don't you take a look?"

Instead of looking at herself, George gazed at Elliot in the mirror.

"What's this?" he asked her. "Don't you trust me?" He leaned down and gently kissed her on her neck. She pulled away from him.

"Well, at least I brought a little color to your cheeks." He grinned at her, then turned and walked to the door. "Madam," he said, offering her his arm.

She tried to sweep past him, but her stomach brushed against him.

"Ah, more color," he said softly.

"Stop it, Elliot," she hissed at him. "I told you I'm not going to play—whatever game this is!"

"You're right," he said easily, as he guided her down the steps toward the dining room. "No games, just breakfast."

They were greeted in the restaurant by the owner of the Brittany Inn, Pietro Cippolo, a rotund, balding man whose Italian accent, Elliot had always thought, was embellished for his guests.

"Ah, dottore Mallory! I saw your name in the register!" He shook Elliot's hand, beaming, and turned to George, a wide smile on his round face. "At last, you and the beautiful *signorina* have become man and wife!"

"Husband and wife," George said acidly, and flushed when she realized what she had said.

Signore Cippolo merely beamed at her. "And a *bambino* on the way! The *dottore* has wasted no time. You will keep your beautiful wife pregnant and safe from all those hungry wolves out there, eh?"

George realized that she had hidden her ring hand in the folds of her jumper. Why, she fumed silently, didn't she just tell the beaming little chauvinist that she and the *dottore* weren't married?

"You come with me," Signore Cippolo said, bowing to George. "We will give you an exquisite breakfast. You and your little one."

"Yes, George," Elliot said, "come along. Let's feed the big one, too."

She turned around to face him, hoping for a jarring insult to come to mind, but when she looked up at him, she couldn't think of thing to say. He was smiling down at her, his eyes so tender that she looked uncomfortably away. She tossed her head and sailed after Signore Cippolo, heeling dangerously close to a table.

Signore Cippolo held her chair out for her with a sweeping bow. "*Signora*," he boomed, "you will stay home now and make babies with your husband? No more television?"

Elliot said quickly, "I would likely be shot, Pietro, if I kept George from her public. She is a new woman, you know. She can take care of her husband and her babies and still leave the world sighing over her beauty on television."

"Ah, no," Pietro said dramatically, poking his finger at his chest. "Me, I would be too jealous to let her into the world. But you are right. The world has changed and our women with it. Here is Maria. She will take your order now. You will drink a glass of healthy milk, Signora George," he added with his beaming smile. "I want your *bambino* to be as handsome and athletic as his father."

"I'm hoping for a *bambina*," George said.

"A *bambina* is just fine with me," Elliot said once Pietro had left their table. He felt absurdly pleased that George hadn't told Pietro they weren't married.

"I would like some French toast, please, Maria," George said to their waitress, ignoring Elliot. "And an order of bacon."

"Make sure it's very crisp, Maria," Elliot said.

George gazed around the intimate dining room with its quaint early American furnishings and its homey atmosphere while Elliot ordered. Why a man as Italian as Mr. Cippolo had elected to adorn his inn with early American antiques escaped her. She had fallen in love with the Brittany Inn when Elliot first brought her here.

"Coffee, George?"

At her nod, he filled her cup from the silver coffeepot on their table.

"Beautiful day," he said.

"Yes."

"Why didn't you tell him we weren't married?"

She grew very still. "There was no point in embarrassing the poor man," she said finally.

"Thank you for sparing him and me such an embarrassment," he said dryly. "Do you really want a *bambina*, George?"

"Being a man, I suppose it would please your vanity to father a son." She caught herself, and added quickly, "I just want a healthy baby."

"Good, so do I. Boy or girl, our child will be quite a jock." She stiffened, her lips drawing in a tight line, and he quickly sought a neutral subject.

"What do you intend to do with Braden-Tyrol? I wondered about your three-year contract with them." When she didn't immediately answer, Elliot continued easily, "I hope you don't mind my asking. It's just curiosity."

She smiled slightly, remembering Ben's shock when she had first told him about the baby. "They weren't too happy about my pregnancy at first," she admitted. "I didn't even know until I was on location at Mount Rushmore in April."

"Mount Rushmore?" he asked. He arched an eyebrow at her in question, though he had seen the commercial on TV. He wanted to keep her talking.

"The point of the commercial was to show that no man, not even one carved in stone, could resist a woman wearing their makeup and perfume. The special effects were clever, I suppose. I flew by in a glider and they turned their heads at me. Oddly enough, it was my makeup man who asked me if I was pregnant." She paused a moment. "I was speechless, as you can well imagine. When Ben told the higher-ups at Braden-Tyrol, they wanted to dump me. I was lucky. They'd gotten a lot of good feedback about me and decided they'd stay with me. My agreement with them is that I'll work steadily for two weeks in November and produce at least three commercials that they'll air immediately. Then, I travel no more than a week each month after that."

"The baby is due in October," Elliot said. "That isn't much time for you to get back on your feet."

"They're more worried about my getting back my figure than my feet," George retorted. "But I'll do it."

"How much weight have you gained so far?"

"About nine pounds. I plan to hold it to fifteen. No more, or I won't have a prayer of looking like anything but a blimp on TV in November."

He hadn't noticed until now that her face was thinner, her high cheekbones more pronounced. She looked fragile, and it took all his resolve to keep his mouth shut.

"How did you get Braden-Tyrol to let you appear pregnant in that fashion magazine?"

She smiled, but said nothing until Maria had set her French toast in front of her. "Clyde, my photographer, was delighted about the baby and insisted on taking pictures of me every single week. It was actually Ben's idea when he saw some of the photos. It so happens that Braden-Tyrol owns subsidiary clothing boutiques. They agreed to let me model their maternity clothes. It worked well, I suppose. Since I was under contract with them, they got my work for free."

They fell silent for a few minutes, eating their breakfast. Elliot thought about the miserable months he had spent, unaware in his misery of what he was missing. He could have seen his baby growing, been with George every day as she changed. He gulped down his coffee.

"Were you sick often?" he asked.

"Very seldom, and then I think it was psychological. I didn't throw up once until I knew for sure I was pregnant."

"You do have a doctor, George?"

"Yes, doctor, I do. Obviously," she continued arply, "she isn't one of your cronies."

He sat back in his chair and folded his arms over his chest. "Do your parents know, George?"

He saw a look of pain cross her face. "I had to tell them. Tod and Mariana live in Mill Valley, and I couldn't just tell them to forget about me until October. And Tod couldn't keep a secret if his fastball depended on it. They are...concerned."

Elliot fiddled with his fork for a few moments. "I suppose I'm surprised that Tod or Mariana or your parents didn't come after me with a shot gun."

"I didn't tell them you were the father."

"I see," he said. "Norman Greenberg?"

She flushed and ducked her head. "No! I told them we had broken up and I had had a weekend fling in Lake Tahoe."

"I see," he said again. "What do you plan to do, George?"

"I think I already told you that, doctor. I will return to work in November. I've already got feelers out for a live-in nurse. It won't be bad once everything is settled. And I don't intend to travel more than once a month, as I said."

"Are you finished with your breakfast?" he asked abruptly.

She nodded.

"Good." He rose and smiled down at her. "It's a beautiful day, George. Let's go for a walk to the beach. I'd like to tell you my plans."

"*Your* plans have nothing to do with me!"

"Let's just go for that walk."

"And then we'll go back to San Francisco?"

"If you wish," he said, lying fluently.

Chapter 18

The Brittany Inn was just off Ocean Avenue and only a ten-minute walk from the beach. George breathed in the clean ocean air as they drew near, and despite herself, she began to relax.

"Would you like to know what I've been doing for the past six months?" Elliot asked, slowing his pace even more so he wouldn't tire her.

"I suppose you'll tell me anyway."

"True. First of all, you're lucky I'm still alive."

He saw a brief look of alarm in her eyes before she managed to quash it. "What do you mean?" she asked carefully, her eyes on her shoes.

"What I mean is that I've become such a mean son of a bitch that if one of my colleagues had put a contract out on me, they'd have given him a medal. It's been...rough, George."

"Sure," she said, "I'll just bet you've had a thoroughly wretched time. Did Eileen Raeburn try to put you out of your misery too?"

"Eileen," he repeated, forgetting who she was for a moment. "No," he said slowly, watching her face carefully, "she had no reason to complain. A woman as pretty as she is hardly ever does."

Elliot saw her press her lips into a tight line, and was pleased. They had reached the end of the path, and he cupped her elbow in his hand. "Let's walk on the sand. Would you like to take your shoes off?"

She nodded, bent over awkwardly and slipped off her heels.

"How about your panty hose?"

She shot him a look of sheer dislike and shook her head. "They're old. It doesn't matter."

"I don't know how your pink panther knee socks are going to look with that dress. I only packed one pair of panty hose."

"It doesn't matter," she repeated. "We're going back to San Francisco today."

"There is that," he said agreeably.

The tide was coming in, and every few feet they had to step back to keep the frothy water from spilling over their feet. There was an awkward silence between them.

"I wish I had thought to bring some toast for the gulls," George said, turning her face skyward at their loud squawking.

Elliot bent down, picked up a knobby stick and flung it into the water. Her eyes were drawn to the play of muscles in his shoulders. He looked so bloody handsome, she thought.

"You've lost weight," she said abruptly, hating herself for the concern in her voice.

"Yes," he said. "Nearly ten pounds."

"You shouldn't have."

He shrugged. "There was little else to do except exhaust myself." He grinned at her. "You'll never beat me swimming now, George."

"It doesn't matter," she said.

He cocked a black brow at her. "Is that going to be your refrain? Your Greek chorus? We'll have to come up with a different line."

She stopped in her tracks and turned to face him. "Listen to me, Elliot," she said. "I don't know why you dragged me down here. I don't understand you. But believe me, I just want to go home."

"Back to your alcohol and cigarettes?"

"That was just a temporary...aberration. I don't want to have another hangover as long as I live."

"Good. I'm delighted. You want to know why I brought you here? I'm ready to tell you if you're ready to listen." ·

She pursed her lips. "Very well. It doesn't appear that I really have much choice in the matter." She sounded bitchy, but she couldn't help it.

"You want the baby now?" he asked. His voice was expressionless, giving her no clue to his feelings.

"Don't be a fool," she said coldly.

"Then it was as I suspected. All that talk about an abortion was just to...rile me?"

"It seems to be hard, if not impossible, to rile you when you're playing at being controlled."

"You riled me, all right," he said softly. "Oh yes, you riled me but good, George." He pointed to some jutting rocks at the end of the cove. "Come sit down for a minute."

She was tired, she thought. Tired from a stupid ten-minute walk on the beach. She sat down on a rock, placed her shoes beside her and folded her hands in her lap. "Talk, doctor," she said.

He stood in front of her, his hands thrust into the pockets of his corduroy jeans. "I guess the first thing I should say is that I was a fool. An ass. I really thought I was saving you from making a grave mistake with your life."

"And my becoming pregnant has changed everything? Elliot, grant me some intelligence!"

"I always have," he said, grinning at her. "What you have done lady, is save me from myself and my outdated nobility."

"Hah! I have done nothing to you, Elliot," she said steadily. *Except love you and ask you to marry me.*

"George, you did everything to me, beginning from the moment you slammed that volleyball in my face last summer. I thought you were the most unusual and beautiful female I'd ever seen. Your Beau Jangles shirt nearly did me in. I wanted to make love with you. And, when we did, finally, I discovered quickly enough that I wanted more, much more. Our age difference didn't really hit me until I realized I was in love with you."

George scrambled up from the rock. "You're a liar!" she yelled, shaking her shoes at him. "So that's it, Elliot! You're ready to marry me now that I'm pregnant. Let me ask you something, Dr. Mallory. Can you tell me honestly that you would ever have willingly seen me again if I weren't pregnant?"

"George, I admit to being a fool and an ass, but I am not a liar, except to myself. God knows all the reasons I broke off with you are still there. The age difference, and your career." He ran distracted fingers through his hair. "Damn, George, I don't know. I really don't."

"Another character trait of your generation, Elliot? Knock up a woman and you're honor-bound to marry her? That's really great—spending your life with someone out of obligation!"

"The baby is my responsibility," he said quietly. "But that isn't the whole of it, and you know it, George. If I didn't love you to distraction, then it would be a case of obligation, I suppose. But I do love you."

"I'm not going to listen to you anymore!" She flung her shoes at him, wheeled about and started running down the beach.

"George!" he shouted after her. "Stop it!"

He caught up with her quickly, just as she stumbled. He caught her and drew her into his arms.

"Let me go!" she yelled against his chest. She tried to strike him, but he held her too tightly.

"No, I won't let you go. Ever again. I love you, and you're right, I did lie to you because I didn't want to see you hurt."

"Hurt?" She threw her head back, and gave him a wild laugh. "Hurt? What the hell do you think I've been doing for the past six months? Dancing around with joy that I was free of you?" She couldn't help it. She felt tears swimming in her eyes, spilling down her cheeks. "How could you do that to me if you really loved me? It's like you were playing a game with me, with my life. I was just one little pawn you moved around to suit you!"

"It was probably the stupidest thing I've ever done. But believe me, George, please...I was convinced that I was doing what was best for you. It was arrogant and wrong of me. But I do love you, George, have loved you for so damned long that living through each day without you has been one constant effort."

She shook her head against his chest, covering her ears with her hands to keep out his words.

"The only way I'll let you go," he whispered wearily against her temple, "is if you tell me you no longer love me."

She became utterly still. Slowly, she raised her face to look at him. "Love you? Don't you mean infatuated with you, Elliot? Don't tell me you're now admitting that I actually felt something more than postteenage romantic feelings for the first man who screwed me?"

He didn't even blink at her show of crudeness, knowing she'd said it because she hurt. Lightly, he ran his fingers over her jaw and gently flicked away her tears. "How come," he said gently, "you're so damned mature at twenty-four and I'm such a jerk at thirty-eight?"

"You're a man," she said, sniffing. "I'm learning that all men have that in common."

He smiled at her and released her arms. She dashed her hand across her eyes, but she didn't retreat from him. "And I've just realized something," he continued after a moment. "If you had called me, particularly during the past couple of months, I would have melted on the phone. But I would have fought against it, George; I won't lie to you." He paused a moment, and drew a deep breath. "If you don't want to marry me, if I've hurt you too much, I'll back off. But I don't want to. I want you and our baby. I want to sleep with you every night and wake up with you every morning. I want to play with you in every sport you can devise. I want to tease you and make love to you. I want to laugh again, George."

She stepped away from him and moved closer to the lapping water. She wrapped her arms about her and stared out over the waves. Without turning, she said, "I'm probably the fool because I want to believe you. With all my heart, I want to believe you. All I have to do is think about you and I melt. But the pain, Elliot. I don't ever want that kind of pain again."

He strode to her and gently clasped her arms, pulling her against his chest. "Nor do I, George. I'll do my best never to hurt you again. Will you marry me? Will you be my lover? Will you spend your life with me?

He felt a shudder go through her body. Very slowly, she nodded.

Elliot wanted to shout; he wanted to sing. Instead, he gently turned her about, drew her into his arms and kissed her very slowly and thoroughly.

"It's been so long," she said softly into his mouth.

"Yes. You know what else I want to do? I want to take you back to our room and make love to you. I want to feel every inch of you, George."

To his surprise, she looked away from him, her eyes lowered.

"What is this? Modesty from my soon-to-be wife?"

She wrung her hands. "I—I look awful!" she blurted out. "I'm so skinny except for my stomach. I look like a spider."

"Then let me step into your parlor."

She laughed; she couldn't help it. "You—you won't mind?"

"Don't be silly," he said tenderly. "I want to feel our baby and stare at your belly for hours. It's my male conceit. You'll have to put up with it. And I want to see that scar of yours. If Greenberg really did an excellent job, I won't go down and murder the man."

There was such pleasure in his voice, such tenderness in his dark eyes, that she wanted to cry again. But he kissed her again, stroked his hands down her back, and she forgot about crying.

"Come on, sweetheart," he said gently. "Will you make love with me?"

She stood on tiptoes and wrapped her arms around his neck. "Where did you lose that ten pounds?" she whispered provocatively in his ear.

He knew she was embarrassed, and therefore went very slowly. When she was finally naked, he stood back and let his eyes wander over every inch of her.

"I love you so much," he said. Lightly, he touched his hand to her belly and caressed her. "My touted control is slipping, George."

She lay on her back on the bed, watching him yank off his clothes. When he turned around to face her, her eyes widened.

"I know what you're thinking," he said, grinning at her.

"How could you?" she protested. "I was just going to reassure you that the ten pounds you lost aren't—"

"Hush, woman. Now I'm the one who's embarrassed. My ribs are showing."

"But I wasn't looking at your ribs, Elliot."

"It appears you've got your wit back. I'm so besotted, I probably won't win an argument for another six months."

He lay down beside her and stared for a long moment at her. Lightly, he touched her breast. "More than a handful now," he said, leaning down to gently kiss her.

"Yes, and it's a nuisance. How can those overly endowed movie stars enjoy carrying all that around?"

"Men," he said, laughing softly. "The more the merrier for some of us blighted specimens. Now, would you please shut up so I can seduce you?"

He was watching her as he spoke, and saw a flicker of uncertainty in her expressive eyes. "What's wrong, sweetheart?"

"I'm scared," she whispered, staring raptly at his collarbone.

His hand roved downward and came to rest on her stomach. "Of what?"

He felt the child move against his hand and laughed delightedly. "Ah, George, what a rowdy little beggar he is. Now, tell me, no more stalling. What scares you?"

"I haven't felt anything in so long," she managed. "I don't know if I can now."

It wouldn't be wise, he decided quickly, to tease her about her mythical lovers. "For me too, George. We've got all the time in the world. All you have to do is relax, and trust me. Okay?"

His eyes locked with hers, and he eased his hand lower. "Familiar territory," he said softly, slowly stroking her. "And just a tiny little scar."

"You—you haven't made love to anyone since us?"

"No. It was too grim a thought."

He felt a gentle stirring in her. "Oh," she gasped. "I'd forgotten."

"Not me," he said ruefully. "I'd lie in bed at night, remembering how you feel, and those soft mewling sounds you'd make in your throat. Do you remember how it felt when we were together?"

"Yes," she whispered. She ran her hands over his chest and ribs, then clasped them behind his back. "I've got to fatten you up."

"On your cooking?" he teased her. "Just smile at me every day and tell me you can't live without me, and I'll fill out in no time at all. Not quite like you, of course, but still…"

She squeezed him as hard as she could, and she felt a deep rumble of laughter in his chest.

He hugged her to him, and kissed her. "George," he said, easing back so he could see her face.

"Hmm?"

"You became pregnant our last night together."

"Yes, it would seem so."

"You weren't using your diaphragm?"

She looked at him doubtfully, a flicker of fear in her eyes.

"No, I'm not about to accuse you of getting pregnant on purpose, idiot. I just wanted to know how virile I am."

She shook her head. "No, I didn't use anything. It was only a couple of days after my period, about the same time of the month we first made love. I didn't think I could get pregnant."

"It must have been fate, then." Elliot raised his eyes toward the ceiling and began to murmur in Latin.

George buffeted him on the shoulder. "You're supposed to be paying attention to me. What are you doing?"

"Praying. Offering up thanksgiving, and promising a life of good works and moral rectitude."

"When you finish, please love me," she whispered, and drew his face down to her.

"I will," he said, drawing her on her side against him. "You can count on that."

The Silhouette Cameo Tote Bag Now available for just $6.99

Handsomely designed in blue and bright pink, its stylish good looks make the Cameo Tote Bag an attractive accessory. The Cameo Tote Bag is big and roomy (13″ square), with reinforced handles and a snap-shut top. You can buy the Cameo Tote Bag for $6.99, plus $1.50 for postage and handling.

Send your name and address with check or money order for $6.99 (plus $1.50 postage and handling), a total of $8.49 to:

Silhouette Books
120 Brighton Road
P.O. Box 5084
Clifton, NJ 07015-5084
ATTN: Tote Bag

SIL-T-1R

The Silhouette Cameo Tote Bag can be purchased pre-paid only. No charges will be accepted. Please allow 4 to 6 weeks for delivery.

N.Y. State Residents Please Add Sales Tax

Offer not available in Canada.

READERS' COMMENTS ON
SILHOUETTE INTIMATE MOMENTS:

"About a month ago a friend loaned me my first Silhouette. I was thoroughly surprised as well as totally addicted. Last week I read a Silhouette Intimate Moments and I was even more pleased. They are the best romance series novels I have ever read. They give much more depth to the plot, characters, and the story is fundamentally realistic. They incorporate tasteful sex scenes, which is a must, especially in the 1980's. I only hope you can publish them fast enough."

S.B.*, Lees Summit, MO

"After noticing the attractive covers on the new line of Silhouette Intimate Moments, I decided to read the inside and discovered that this new line was more in the line of books that I like to read. I do want to say I enjoyed the books because they are so realistic and a lot more truthful than so many romance books today."

J.C., Onekama, MI

"I would like to compliment you on your books. I will continue to purchase all of the Silhouette Intimate Moments. They are your best line of books that I have had the pleasure of reading."

S.M., Billings, MT

*names available on request

Silhouette Books

*brings you the best
in contemporary romance.*

SILHOUETTE ROMANCE—
contemporary romances that depict all the
wonder and magic of falling in love.

SILHOUETTE DESIRE—more sensual,
provocative stories of modern women in
realistic situations.

SILHOUETTE SPECIAL EDITION—
longer contemporary romances,
emphasizing emotion as well as heightened
romantic tension. And SILHOUETTE
SPECIAL EDITIONs are sensuous and
believable love stories.

AND NOW

SILHOUETTE INTIMATE MOMENTS—
love stories with the one element no one
else has tapped: excitement. They are
longer, more sensuous romance novels
filled with adventure, suspense, glamour
or melodrama.